## He could not sate his desire for Megan Wells

She was vulnerable. Needy. Still grieving over her dead husband. But terror had swept over him when he'd seen her car on fire. For a minute, he'd thought she might be dead.

Where had this desperate fear, this insatiable desire come from?

Images suddenly bombarded him. Images of another time when Megan had readily slipped into his arms. A warm spring day when they had walked naked into the ocean, laughing and teasing like old lovers. A night when he hadn't needed an invitation to kiss her.

How could he see these things so vividly in his mind when he couldn't remember anything about his life? When the name Cole Hunter still sounded foreign to his tongue? When Megan swore they had never met?

Could the doctors have made some mistake in identifying him?

Dear Harlequin Intrigue Reader,

Deck the halls with romance and suspense as we bring you four new stories that will wrap you up tighter than a present under your Christmas tree!

First we begin with the continuing series by Rita Herron, NIGHTHAWK ISLAND, where medical experiments on an island off the coast of Georgia lead to some dangerous results. Cole Hunter does not know who he is, and the only memories he has are of Megan Wells's dead husband. And why does he have these intimate *Memories of Megan*?

Next, Susan Kearney finishes her trilogy THE CROWN AFFAIR, which features the Zared royalty and the treachery they must confront in order to save their homeland. In book three, a prickly, pretty P.I. must pose as a prince's wife in order to help his majesty uncover a deadly plot. However, will she be able to elude his *Royal Pursuit* of her heart?

In Charlotte Douglas's *The Bride's Rescuer*, a recluse saves a woman who washes up on his lonely island, clothed only in a tattered wedding dress. Cameron Alexander hasn't seen a woman in over six years, and Celia Stevens is definitely a woman, with secrets of her own. But whose secrets are more deadly? And also join Jean Barrett for another tale with the Hawke Family Detective Agency in the Christmastime cross-country journey titled *Official Escort*.

Best wishes to all of our loyal readers for a "breathtaking" holiday season!

Sincerely,

Denise O'Sullivan
Associate Senior Editor
Harlequin Intrigue

# MEMORIES OF MEGAN
## RITA HERRON

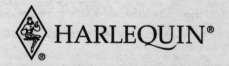

TORONTO • NEW YORK • LONDON
AMSTERDAM • PARIS • SYDNEY • HAMBURG
STOCKHOLM • ATHENS • TOKYO • MILAN • MADRID
PRAGUE • WARSAW • BUDAPEST • AUCKLAND

ISBN 0-373-22689-6

MEMORIES OF MEGAN

**Printed in U.S.A.**

## ABOUT THE AUTHOR

Award-winning author Rita Herron wrote her first book when she was twelve, but didn't think real people grew up to be writers. Now she writes so she doesn't have to get a *real* job. A former kindergarten teacher and workshop leader, she traded her storytelling for kids for romance, and writes romantic comedies and romantic suspense. She lives in Georgia with her own romance hero and three kids. She loves to hear from readers, so please write her at P.O. Box 921225, Norcross, GA 30092-1225 or visit her Web site at www.ritaherron.com.

## Books by Rita Herron

HARLEQUIN INTRIGUE
486—SEND ME A HERO
523—HER EYEWITNESS
556—FORGOTTEN LULLABY
601—SAVING HIS SON
660—SILENT SURRENDER†
689—MEMORIES OF MEGAN†

HARLEQUIN AMERICAN ROMANCE
820—HIS-AND-HERS TWINS
859—HAVE GOWN, NEED GROOM*
872—HAVE BABY, NEED BEAU*
883—HAVE HUSBAND, NEED HONEYMOON*
944—THE RANCHER WORE SUITS

*The Hartwell Hope Chests
†Nighthawk Island

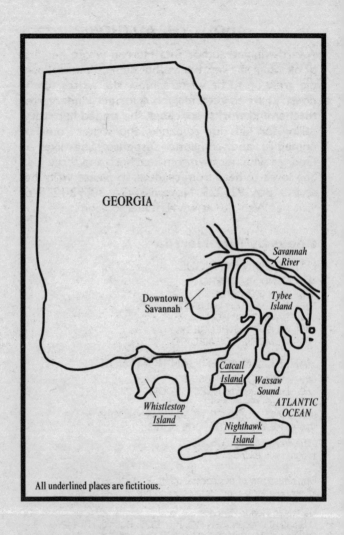

GEORGIA

Savannah River

Downtown Savannah

Tybee Island

Catcall Island

Wassaw Sound

ATLANTIC OCEAN

Whistlestop Island

Nighthawk Island

All underlined places are fictitious.

# CAST OF CHARACTERS

*Megan Wells*—A psychiatric nurse who just lost her husband, Tom. Was his death an accident or murder?

*Tom Wells*—A psychiatrist at the Coastal Island Research Park who lived for his work. Did he die for it, as well?

*Clay Fox*—A detective with the Savannah Police Department. He was supposed to meet Tom Wells to get inside information about the research foundation. Was the psychiatrist murdered for his mission?

*Cole Hunter*—A man with a new face and no memory who has taken Tom Wells's place at the research center. Will he take his place with his wife also?

*Dr. Davis Jones*—A doctor at the foundation; he loves women, money and prestige, and will do anything to attain them. But would he commit murder?

*Dr. Warner Parnell*—A brilliant doctor—is he crossing the line with his medical techniques?

*Arnold Hughes*—The CEO and cofounder of the Coastal Research Park—is he really dead or has he returned with a new face and name to run the company?

*April Conway*—Megan's best friend—or is she?

*Connie Blalock*—Tom's secretary—is she as innocent as she seems?

*Daryl Boyd*—A schizophrenic patient who claims strange things are happening in the psych ward—is he really as crazy as everyone thinks?

To

All those real-life doctors and researchers
who strive to make the world a better place
(this series is NOT about you!)

and

my husband, Lee,
for being one of those doctors,
and for always stopping to answer my questions

and
last but not least,

Melissa Endlich
for liking my crazy ideas instead of calling the funny farm!

Always, Rita

# *Chapter One*

"Your husband is dead, Mrs. Wells." Detective Larson sat down in the armchair across from Megan, his expression grave. "His body washed up on the shore a few hours ago."

Megan clutched her abdomen, the horror of finally hearing her fears confirmed seeping through her body like a slow-spreading virus. It had been six agonizing weeks since Tom had disappeared. Six weeks of not knowing.

Nausea rose to Megan's throat at the images that speared her. She dropped her head forward into her hands and tried to breathe.

"I'll get you a glass of water."

Megan nodded, too numb to do anything else, while the detective hurried to the kitchen.

Behind her, Megan heard the officer opening cabinet doors, turning on the faucet, but the sounds barely registered. Seconds later, he returned and handed her the glass. Megan sipped slowly, grateful for the wetness soothing her parched throat. "Do you know what happened to him?"

The cop's muddy complexion paled as if he, too, had

seen the grisly images that had come unbidden to Megan's mind. Had he been there when they'd dragged her husband from the sea and actually seen Tom's body? The ice clinked in the glass as Megan's hands shook. She didn't want to know the details.

"Most likely drowned, but the coroner's doing an autopsy." Detective Larson shrugged. "I'm not sure how much he'll be able to determine…"

He let the sentence trail off and Megan clenched the glass of water as if it were a life jacket and she was being dragged into the undertow herself.

"You said he liked to fish sometimes, to take his mind off his work. My first guess would be that he was out late, and didn't realize how far he'd drifted off shore, got caught in the tides and fell overboard."

Megan's gaze swung to his. "But Tom was an excellent swimmer."

"You know how difficult it is to fight an undercurrent, even for the best of swimmers. A bad thunderstorm came through that night, too."

She nodded, silently admitting Tom had been drinking a lot those last few weeks, and had been a daredevil when it came to the weather. He'd been drinking *and* secretive. And tired. And disturbed about something. Only he wouldn't talk to her.

She'd known he was unhappy. Had worried he'd stopped loving her, that he'd planned to ask for a divorce, but hadn't gotten up the nerve. They had finally separated, but she'd hoped they could work out their differences.

Now she would never know.

But she couldn't bring herself to ask the questions that had haunted her for the past six weeks.

The detective shuffled, his breathing noisy. "We'll let you know as soon as the body is released so you can make plans for the burial."

Oh, God, there would be so much to do. Nausea gripped her stomach again. She'd have to make funeral arrangements. Tell his parents. The people at the research foundation.

Tom had been so young. Barely thirty-one. They'd only been married two years. They'd temporarily sublet this flat because they hadn't decided for sure where they were going to live. They'd had so many plans when they'd married.

They'd picked out new furniture, not burial plots.

The cop gently patted her shoulder. "Well, let me know if I can do anything for you, Mrs. Wells I'll let myself out."

"Thank you."

She hugged her arms around her middle until she heard the click of the door, and the police car drive away. Finally she forced herself to stand on unsteady legs. But her stomach convulsed and she rushed to the bathroom, sank to her knees and let the tears fall.

The pregnancy test she'd taken earlier mocked her from the sink.

It had been negative. Again. Tom had wanted a baby so badly. She'd felt like a failure when their attempts at conceiving had failed.

Now he would never have a child.

And she had nothing left of him but troubled memories.

And questions. Lots of unanswered questions.

"YOU SAID MY NAME WAS WHAT?" The man pivoted to study the doctor as he unwound the last of the ban-

dages from his face. He was too afraid of what he might
see when the last one fell away.

Dr. Crane peered over his silver spectacles, worry
creasing his brow. "Cole Hunter. You're a psychiatrist.
You've just signed on at the Coastal Island Research
Park on Catcall Island. You are—"

"Yeah, yeah, you told me. Thirty-five, single, a
workaholic." Frustration clawed at him. "So, why can't
I remember all this?"

"Because you suffered severe head trauma in the car
accident. Your memory should return in bits and pieces.
Hopefully you haven't lost that scientific mind."

The doctor chuckled at his own joke, but Cole remained stoic. Nothing about the past few weeks had
been funny.

He strained for the memories again, for any snippet
of his past life. Cole Hunter. A psychiatrist. Somehow
during all those painful hours of lying in the hospital
he hadn't imagined himself being a doctor of any kind.

Of course, until a few days ago he'd been in too
much pain to care about the past. He'd been struggling
through every minute. The long hospital stay, the sur-
geries, the bandages. The fear of not waking up. The
fear of being paralyzed. The fear of looking like a mon-
ster.

"Now, see what modern medicine can do." Dr.
Crane spun the stool around so Cole faced the mirror,
placed his hands on Cole's shoulders and directed him
to look. "It may not be quite the same as your old face,
but it's not bad. There's a little swelling and bruising,
but it'll fade."

Cole stared at the stranger in the mirror, cold terror

sweeping over him. Not only did he not remember his name, but he didn't recognize the face staring back at him, either.

THREE DAYS AFTER MEGAN had received the news of her husband's death, she stood huddled in her raincoat while they lowered his body into the cold damp ground. Nearly a hundred flower arrangements decorated the dried grass surrounding the grave, their vibrant colors at odds with the dismal day. The church had been packed with Tom's family and their friends, with various scientists and other employees from the Coastal Island Research Park (CIRP). The preacher offered a few words of comfort, read some scripture, then ended the grave side service with a prayer. Tom's mother dropped a rose onto the grave and broke into sobs, her husband pulling her into his arms. Megan's heart clenched as the visitors began to disperse.

A breeze stirred the trees surrounding the cemetery, dead fall leaves scattering across the grass and flapping against tombstones, crunching beneath the soles of people's shoes as they milled about, speaking in hushed tones. Connie, Tom's secretary, cried into her hands.

Exhaustion pulled at Megan as the visitors offered condolences, but she forced herself to shake hands, occasionally sparing her best friend April a glance, silently thanking her for staying by her side, offering support.

Tom's parents had been anything but supportive, their anger over their loss directed at her, as if by marrying Tom she had caused his death. Of course they never had been logical where she was concerned. She was a measly nurse at the research facility, had grown up on the wrong side of the social tracks and had never been good enough, beautiful enough or classy enough for their precious son.

But at least they'd handled most of the details of the funeral. They'd *wanted* to choose the casket, the flowers that would serve as the blanket cover and to oversee the myriad details, while all she'd wanted to do was curl up in a ball and grieve.

Connie suddenly stood in front of her, looking lost. "Meg—" Her voice broke.

Megan pulled her into her arms and tried to soothe her. "It'll be okay, Connie."

"But you and Tom have been so good to me. I don't know what I would have done...what I'll do."

Tom had helped Connie get up the courage to leave her abusive husband. She was still fragile.

"Just know Tom would be proud of you for taking care of your son," Megan said softly. "And he'd want you to be strong, to keep doing that."

Connie pulled away, trying to compose herself, and nodded. "If you need me, Megan, I'm here."

Megan thanked her, weariness settling in her bones as Connie turned and walked away. The long line of people wanting to speak to her stretched in front of her and she felt herself sway.

April grabbed her elbow. "Here, you'd better sit down."

Megan nodded dumbly and sank into a metal folding chair, the sea of people blurring in front of her. Tears streamed down her cheeks, mingling with the rain. She didn't want to be here amidst this crowd of strangers. She wanted to be alone to mourn. Oh, God, there were so many things to mourn for.

The marriage that should have lasted forever.

The man who had died before she could make him happy.

The chance to make things right that was lost forever.

COLE HUNTER WATCHED the casket being lowered into the ground, a bitter chill engulfing him. Oddly, Tom Wells had turned up missing the same day Cole had had his own accident. It could have been his body being lowered into that hole just as easily as Wells.

And for a brief second when he'd seen the casket and the hole in the ground, he'd had a flash that it was him being lowered. That *he* was Tom Wells and he had died.

Warner Parnell, the doctor at the research center who'd been helping Cole with his recovery after the accident, frowned solemnly. "He was a good man. We'll miss him at the center."

"It…it seems strange that I survived, but he died on the same day."

Parnell gave him a sympathetic look. "Don't succumb to survivor guilt," he said in a low voice. "As a doctor, you know that's dangerous."

Cole folded his hands. The harsh reality of the timing obviously hadn't escaped him and had played with his head. He *had* felt guilty that luck had been on his side that day and he had survived. Granted he had a new face, his memory was shaky and his stride hindered by a slight limp, but hell, at least he was still able to walk.

He shuddered, wondering if he should have come. He hadn't wanted to. In fact, he had the oddest feeling that he normally didn't attend funerals, but he couldn't remember why. He'd hoped seeing so many of the research center's staff in one place might jog some memory cells.

"I didn't know him very well, did I?"

Parnell shrugged. "No. You met only once. At the center when you came for the interview. I believe you corresponded through e-mail about your research, but I'm not certain."

Shaking off the uneasy feeling, Cole stared across the smattering of faces, a few of them familiar from the three days he'd spent getting acquainted with the research center.

His gaze settled on Tom Wells's wife. Megan.

A nurse in the psychiatric ward.

Another eerie sensation skittered across his nerve endings, a flash of some kind of memory tugging at him. He must have met her before, probably at the facility or at one of the dinners for the center when he was being interviewed. She wouldn't be an easy woman to forget.

She had the face of an angel, the figure of a temptress and the lips of a lover.

But he had no right to even think such lurid thoughts, especially at a funeral.

From her grief-stricken face, she'd obviously cared for her husband deeply.

During those long, lonely days in the hospital, he had thought about his life, the fact that he had no one. No family who'd come looking for him. No woman who searched him out, sat by his bedside, vowed that she loved him.

Apparently he hadn't made any friends in Oakland, either.

In a strange way, he envied Tom Wells.

He knew that was sick. The poor man was dead, for

God's sake, and here he stood, alive and breathing, feeling sorry for himself.

One by one, the visitors stopped to speak to Megan.

"I'm going to give her my condolences," Parnell said.

Cole hesitated. Finally he took a deep breath and shuffled across the damp ground through the throng of people. Her gaze rose and met his across the crowd. Raindrops dotted her face, mingling with tears, the raincoat shielding her honey-colored hair and shapely body. But it was the shadows beneath her haunted blue eyes that made his gut clench.

An older man and woman Parnell had pointed out as Wells's parents stopped beside her. Megan stiffened, clasping her hands tightly together. Cole moved into the shadows of the funeral home tent, close enough to hear.

"You will send us Tom's things, won't you?" the woman asked in a clipped voice.

"Yes, if you want them."

"Of course we do." Mrs. Wells flashed Megan a cold look. "He never should have come here, you know."

Megan jutted her chin in the air. "I'm not going to argue with you at Tom's funeral. I don't think he'd want that, Kathleen."

Mr. Wells pulled at his designer tie. "Let's go, honey." He threw a sorrowful glance over his shoulder at the grave. "There's nothing more we can do."

The couple strode off, huddled together. Hurt strained Megan's features. A fleeting feeling that he'd lived that moment before struck Cole, then disappeared as quickly as it had hit him.

Without remembering how he reached her, Cole found himself standing in front of her, not knowing what to say, but extending his hand, wanting to take away the sting of the Wells's attitude.

She slowly lifted her small hand and placed it inside his, the whisper of her soft skin brushing his callused fingertips. A small surge of awareness skated through him. Her lips parted slightly as if she, too, felt the odd connection between them.

A wave of images suddenly flashed through his head like a movie trailer. Images of Megan Wells looking at him with those haunted blue eyes. Images of her crying on his shoulder. Images of her raising on tiptoe to smother his mouth with kisses. Images of her lying naked in his arms and calling his name in the darkness of the night.

He snapped his hand back and felt himself grow weak. What in the hell had just happened? Those flashes seemed so real. But they couldn't have been memories.

Could they?

## Chapter Two

Megan's hand trembled as she pulled it from the stranger's, a slight chill slithering up her spine. She pulled her raincoat around her, trying to place his face in the fog of grief engulfing her, yet she had never met him before. Or had she?

And why was he looking at her so intensely?

"I'm sorry about your husband," he said in a gruff voice. "I'm afraid I didn't know him very well—I'd just been hired to work at the center."

He was nervous, she realized, remembering that Tom had an aversion to funerals as well. Maybe it was a man thing. Not that she enjoyed going to them herself, but sometimes people didn't have a choice. In fact, she'd already been to enough funerals to last a lifetime.

At ten she had lost her only grandparents. At seventeen, she'd buried her parents.

And now Tom.

She shook her head, operating on autopilot. "Thank you for coming, Mr...."

"Hunter. Cole Hunter." A frown pinched his dark eyebrows as he shifted. "Anyway, I just wanted to offer my regrets."

Megan nodded, clasping her hands together as his dark eyes bore into hers. "I suppose I'll see you at the center."

"I suppose." He lifted his hand to wipe away the raindrops sliding down his cheek. A long scar curved his hand, another smaller one darkened his hairline. She wondered what had happened to him, but forced herself not to ask. Tom's mother claimed she'd grown up on the wrong side of the tracks of Savannah, but even in shanty town, Megan had been taught manners.

"Yes. As a matter of fact, we'll be working together." His voice lowered, sympathy etching it with gruffness. "That is, when you feel like returning to work."

Megan nodded. She hadn't thought that far ahead. Then again, work would probably fill the endless, empty days ahead. Help take her mind off of her grief. And her patients' problems were so troubling they usually made hers feel trivial. Except Tom's death wasn't trivial. "You're in psychiatry?"

His dark eyes looked somber. "Yes."

For the first time, Megan realized he was handsome. Not in the gentlemanly way Tom had been, but in a more rugged way. He was big and muscular; he stood about six foot two, had broad shoulders, and a wide strong jaw.

Guilt suffused her—how could she notice a man's looks when Tom had just been put in the ground? What kind of wife was she? Had she been?

One who had disappointed her husband…

Cole Hunter shifted again, wincing as if his leg hurt. He was leaning on a dark wooden cane. So, he had been hurt recently. The reason for the scars, perhaps the reason he was so lean...

"I was actually coming to work with Tom."

Megan's throat closed. A dozen other questions tumbled through her head, but the realization that she would see this man again, and probably on a daily basis, shook her to the core.

The trouble was she had no idea why the idea upset her so. She only knew that she didn't want to be around him. And that the eerie feeling she'd had when they'd first met had just magnified tenfold.

COLE STEPPED BACK AS MEGAN stood to leave, and offered a hand for support, but she refused his help, looking wary as if he'd said or done something to upset her. Odd, how just a few moments before he'd met her, he'd had visions of knowing her, of seeing her before, when now his mind almost seemed blank. Like a deep tunnel, long and empty and devastatingly dark.

Briefly he wondered if they could have had an affair.

No, she hadn't acted as if she'd known him at all.

Of course, his face looked different, but if they'd known each other before, if they'd met, she would have recognized his name.

Instincts told him he wasn't the kind of man to sleep with another man's wife.

Or was he?

Confused, he hunched inside his jacket and followed the other mourners. God, he hated that damned cane. A tall redhead gathered Megan Wells into a protective embrace. Obviously a close friend, Megan leaned on the other woman as if she were exhausted. He imagined she was. His own muscles protested the long walk. He hated the weakness right now. Hated any kind of weakness.

The light rain drizzled down, the fall wind kicking up, stirring wet leaves and forcing the flowers from other graves to sway and droop as he limped across the grass.

Parnell turned to wait for him at the edge of the cemetery. "How's the leg?"

Cole grimaced. "Getting better." He squinted through the hazy sky as Megan and her friend climbed in the car. "Have I met Mrs. Wells before?"

"Not that I know of." Parnell frowned and pulled out his keys. "Why do you ask?"

Cole shrugged. "I don't know. She just seems... familiar."

"You probably saw a picture of Tom and her somewhere. I believe he's got one in his office."

Cole chuckled softly. "Probably."

"Get some rest. I'll see you at the center."

Cole flicked his hand in a wave as Parnell jogged to his car. Cole couldn't move quite so fast. The scent of sorrow and dank muddy ground assailed him as he headed down the embankment. He dreaded going back to his place.

The small apartment at the edge of the research center didn't hold a damn bit of recognition for him. A place he'd been told he'd agreed to rent when he signed on with CIRP and made his transition from...where did they say he'd come from? Some little research hospital in the foothills of Tennessee?

But he remembered none of it. And the apartment he'd chosen to live in didn't feel like home at all. It felt like a prison.

MEGAN SET THE CUP OF TEA on the kitchen table and folded her hands in her lap. "Thanks, April. I don't know what I would have done without you the last three days. Please tell all the nurses and staff members how much I appreciate the food they brought." Casseroles and homemade dishes filled the butcher block counter. So much food. Food she had no appetite for.

"Who was that man talking to you before you left?" April asked.

Megan blew into the tea to cool it. "His name is Cole Hunter. He's a new psychiatrist at the center."

Sympathy filled April's eyes. "It looked as if he upset you."

Megan shrugged. "He came here to work with Tom." She didn't want to tell her the rest, how his touch had given her the strangest feeling. How just looking into his eyes had been unnerving. April would think she was crazy.

"I'm so sorry, Meg." April leaned over and hugged her. "I know how much you wanted things to work out for you and Tom."

Megan nodded, warming her hands on the oversize mug and rolling her shoulders. Tension clawed at her, the lack of sleep and emotions over the past few days finally wearing her down.

"You look exhausted. Drink that and get some rest." April grabbed her raincoat. "And call me if you need me."

"I will. You be careful." Megan rose and latched the lock on her front door, her eyes narrowing when she glanced out the window and watched April sprint to her car. Seconds later, April climbed in her Volvo and drove away, rain spewing from the back of her car as she sped toward the cottage she rented on Skidaway Island. Megan let the curtain slip back in place, but a dark sedan across the street drew her eye. It was parked in the shadows of a live oak, the Spanish moss drooping like spider legs, casting it in shadows made worse by the dark sky. She peeled the curtain back and studied the vehicle for a moment, trying to see if someone was inside. Was a cigarette glowing from the interior? Had she seen the car in the neighborhood before? Could it belong to one of her neighbors? People she'd never met because she and Tom had both been too busy at work to entertain? Too busy trying to hold their marriage together?

Except for those last few weeks when he'd moved out, when she sensed he'd given up...

Had she seen the car while he was gone?

After several tense seconds, she decided she must be getting paranoid. The car was empty. And there was no reason for anyone to be lurking outside her apartment. No reason anyone would follow her or want to harm her. After all, Tom's death had been accidental, not suspicious.

Chuckling at her runaway imagination, she carried her tea to the bedroom, bypassing Tom's closet with a tentative glance. At some point she had to sort through his things and clear them out. At least what he hadn't taken with him when they'd separated.

But not tonight. She was too battered by Tom's funeral.

She slipped beneath the covers and finished the tea, grateful for the small shot of bourbon April had laced it with. Weariness pulled at her, but the uneasiness she'd felt earlier rose again to taunt her. Could someone have been outside watching her? And if they had, who were they?

She couldn't quite forget the trouble surrounding Nighthawk Island and the research center just a few short weeks ago. That Arnold Hughes, the CEO and co-founder who'd been behind the unsavory sale of some of their research, might not be dead as the police hoped. That his body had never been found.

That Tom had been working on something secretive the last few months, something that had made him jittery and even more closed off from her than before. And that a stranger had been at Tom's funeral. A man who had recently been in an accident of some kind himself but who'd taken her husband's place at the hospital.

A man who had come out of nowhere.

COLE WALKED THE OUTER BANKS surrounding the research center on Skidaway Island, amidst the tall sea oats and damp grass, well aware security tracked his every move. He inhaled the scent of ocean, needing the familiarity, because nothing else about his life seemed remotely familiar.

Not the idea of being a psychiatrist or the people he'd met at the funeral or the little apartment he'd returned home to.

Home.

What did it mean for him? He had no friends. No family. Not even back in Tennessee where Davis Jones, the head of the psychiatric ward had told him he'd moved from. Hell, Jones had even shown him his résumé, but the information on it seemed foreign as well. Apparently he'd gone to Vanderbilt, worked at a small private practice before signing on with the research facility in Oakland.

Wind whistled through the sea oats, a seagull swooped onto the shore in search of crumbs, and water lapped at the shore in a soothing rhythm. The doctor warned that it would take time to recover his memories. The sea stretched before him, endless and all consuming, just as the blank spaces in his mind. How much time would it take to recover? Would his memory ever fully return? Would he ever feel like the real Cole Hunter again?

An image of Megan Wells's grief-stricken face flashed into his mind, emotions gripping him. If they had never met, why had he experienced visions of her when he'd touched her?

HE WAS WATCHING HER. Standing beside her bed, his dark eyes staring at her, his hand outstretched.

Shadows hugged the walls, the curtain billowing out from the window, the whisper of a familiar scent filling the room. His cologne. The one she had given him for Christmas last year.

The one he'd hated.

Megan struggled to reach for his hand but her arm was too heavy. Frustration welled inside her. She focused her energy on lifting her hand, but just as she did, he took a step backward. His frame stood silhouetted in the moonlight, the dark look of concern on his face so somber, a whimper bubbled in her throat.

What was wrong?

It was Tom, wasn't it?

He opened his mouth as if to speak, his eyebrows pinched the way they did when he was trying to concentrate. But when he opened his mouth, no sound came out. She tried to reach for him again, but he slipped farther away, almost floating now, the distance sucking him in some kind of surreal vacuum... What was he trying to tell her?

"Don't go," she whispered. "Please, don't leave me."

His lips moved again, slowly as if it were painful, and she traced the movements, studying the words. "Be careful, Megan. Don't trust anyone."

Megan jerked upright, her heart pounding. Throwing back the covers, she searched the darkness, a gasp escaping her when she saw the curtain fluttering from the opened window.

Someone had been in her bedroom.

The window had been closed when she'd gone to bed.

HE HUNKERED LOW IN THE CAR, hiding in the shadows of the giant live oak, his only light the cigarette glow in the dim interior of the car. His gaze latched onto Megan Wells's house while he pressed his cell phone to one ear.

"How did the funeral go?"

He snorted. "It was a funeral. How the hell do you think it went?"

His partner chuckled. "Do you think she suspects anything?"

"No, leastways she's not asking any questions." He took a drag from the cigarette, savored the nicotine taste, then blew a smoke ring into the air and watched it swirl in front of him. With a gloved hand, he wiped the fog from the tinted window. A light flickered on in

Megan's bedroom. She was awake now. Probably sitting up in bed, that blond hair tousled around her cheeks, her nightgown clinging to her supple body.

"Good, keep it that way."

He jerked his thoughts back on track. Back to the scene at the graveyard. "But—"

"But what?"

"That guy Hunter, he talked to her for a few minutes after the service."

A long tense silence followed. "What did they talk about?"

"Nothing really. Just chitchat, but he kept watching her, sort of creepy, if you know what I mean."

"Like a man wanting a lay, probably. She is good-looking."

Worry knotted his stomach. Megan Wells was a sharp nurse, intuitive, sensitive to her patients' needs. Smart. Maybe too smart. He shrugged off the worry. "Yeah, I guess that was it." He remembered the way Megan Wells's long blond hair had looked spread across her pillow. Imagined the silky blond strands wound around the black leather of his glove. Damn right she was good-looking.

Unfortunately her good looks wouldn't matter if she started asking questions.

# Chapter Three

Megan's heart pounded as she switched on the light and grabbed the cordless phone. She had to search the apartment.

Sliding from the bed, she reached for the umbrella on the desk, planning to use it as a weapon if necessary. Praying she wouldn't need it, she inched through the room, pausing every few feet to listen for an intruder, but silence hung in the air, deathly calm and frightening.

Her fingers tightened around the umbrella base as she rushed to close the window. On guarded feet, she tiptoed to the doorway and peered into the hallway. Nothing but shadowy blank walls. She took a tentative step, then crept down the hall and checked the small den. Darkness bathed the area, cloaking it in heavy shadows, the leaves of the ficus plant in the corner spearing the wall like thready fingers ready to grab her.

The floor lamp looked ominous, the sofa, the closet, every small crevice a possible hiding place. Taking a deep breath, she flicked on the light, and braced herself. Thankfully her apartment was laid out as one open room, so she could see both the kitchen and den at once. Her gaze searched the parameters. Nothing. She sucked in a deep breath and tiptoed around the corner, then checked underneath the breakfast counter. Again nothing.

Thank God. Adrenaline surged through her as she ran to the door and checked the locks, the windows, the closet. But everything remained intact. No spooky demons or monsters hiding inside or beneath anything.

Her breathing still unsteady, she crept back to the bedroom and stared at the room. The deep maroon walls looked almost bloodlike, the shadows of the tree limbs ominous. She had once thought the room a cozy sanctuary for her and Tom.

Now it seemed frightening. She glanced outside for the dark sedan, rubbing her hands up and down her arms. The car was gone. Still, someone had been inside her house.

Should she call the police? And tell them what? That she thought someone had been in the house because her window was open?

Or had she just imagined that someone had been there? Had she been dreaming of Tom? But what about the faint scent of a man's cologne lingering in the room? Was she imagining that, too?

Stumbling back to bed, she reminded herself how safe she had felt when she and Tom had moved in.

Now she felt anything but safe.

MONDAY MORNING, COLE stepped inside the research center on Catcall Island, feeling lost. His leg throbbed and he leaned on the cane in disgust. He needed a good run, some vigorous exercise to release his tension, but running was definitely out of the question. And the exercises he did to strengthen his leg were painful, slow and frustrating as hell.

"Good morning, Dr. Hunter. I'm Connie, your secretary."

He offered a strained smile. Had he met her?

"I worked for Dr. Wells."

"I...I'm sorry about your boss."

She gestured toward Wells's office, which adjoined hers, although each had separate entrances to the hall as well. "I'm afraid Dr. Wells didn't get a chance to tell me much about you, but welcome to the center."

"Thanks." Unfortunately he couldn't tell her much, either.

"If you need anything, just let me know." She backed toward her desk where he noticed the computer. "Dr. Parnell mentioned that you won't be seeing patients for a while."

"That's right. I need time to get acquainted with things." He pushed open the door to Wells's office. *His* new office. "But thanks for the offer."

"The delivery man brought in your boxes already."

Great. Only he had no idea what was in them.

He stepped inside, scanning the space. The office seemed familiar, yet foreign at the same time. Propping the cane beside the desk, he stretched out his leg and began to rifle though the desk. The next few hours, he searched his memory for anything to jog his mind as he unpacked the stacks of research books and material he had been told belonged to him. Books and notes on schizophrenia, bipolar disorders, hypnosis, manic depression and every mental disorder known to man filled the boxes. He thumbed through each one, frowning at some of the technical jargon. Was he supposedly a specialist on one particular disorder? And if so, why didn't any of the material ring a bell in his foggy brain?

Hopefully they would, he told himself, he just had to be patient. Be patient and move through the days, settling in and familiarizing himself with the routine, the research center, with the work Tom Wells had been doing. Wells's own books and research manuals cluttered the bookcases on one wall, the materials piled haphazardly as if in no particular order. A small oval plastic cup overflowed with paper clips, shredded paper filled the trash can, and a coffee stain darkened the sleek black top of the desk. The man obviously hadn't been obsessive compulsive about neatness.

Except that all his notes were typed, not handwritten. Probably couldn't read his own writing.

He halted, wondering how he had made that deduction. Was it the first sign that he was a psychiatrist? It was a small tidbit but he clung to it. Now what should he do?

A silver-framed five-by-seven photo of Megan Wells and her husband occupied the corner of the desk. His gut clenched at the ghostly feeling that encompassed him.

She wore a pale blue sundress that accentuated her eyes, he wore a white polo shirt and khaki shorts. Tom's arm was thrown around his wife's shoulders, wind whipped through their hair, sails flapped in the breeze, and the bright sun gleamed off their smiles. They had looked amazingly happy.

He didn't think he was normally an emotional man, but it seemed like a betrayal to Wells's memory for him to move into his space so soon after his death. To take over his office and discard his personal things. To put

Wells's wife's photo aside and add one of his own. Not that he had any personal photos to add.

But Jones had insisted that Tom would have wanted his work to continue, that Tom lived for his research and prided himself on his commitment to his profession and his patients.

What about his wife? Had Wells been a doting husband or had he been so obsessed with his work that she had taken second place?

He shook away the troubling thought, wondering why he had even given it a moment's interest. Megan Wells had looked happy in the photo. And she had been grief-stricken at her husband's funeral. Besides, she was not his problem.

God knew he had enough of his own.

Still, so far the memories of her had been more tangible than any others.

Maybe she held some secret key that might unlock his past.

MEGAN ENTERED THE RESEARCH center hospital area through the security checkpoint, stopping only to accept brief offers of sympathy from various employees.

"I'm surprised to see you here," Doris, one of the young research assistants said.

"It's better to keep busy." Megan moved on for fear of breaking down. Several of the other staff members echoed the same sentiment as she veered down the corridor toward Tom's office.

Two of Tom's colleagues, Davis Jones and Warner Parnell, seemed engrossed in a serious discussion as they approached her from the opposite direction. Something about the case study on autism treatments, she heard one of them say. But as soon as they spotted her, the conversation instantly died.

"We didn't expect you to come back to work so soon." Dr. Jones, a handsome man in his early forties with thick tawny hair and a tanned complexion, met her in the hall in front of Tom's secretary's office. Through the crack in the doorway, Megan saw Connie stooped over the computer.

"I'm not officially on duty," Megan explained. "So I thought I'd come and clean out Tom's office." She hadn't been able to touch his personal things at home yet.

Dr. Parnell, an older gray-haired gentlemen with thick dark glasses nodded. "Probably a good idea."

"Let me know if I can help, Megan," Dr. Jones said.

Megan nodded, anxious to escape the doctors. Davis Jones had always made her uncomfortable. Both his cocky smile and his reputation with the ladies raised her defenses fast. She'd observed Dr. Parnell at work with some of the schizophrenic patients. He could be kind and sympathetic, yet ruthless when dealing with a disgruntled patient who refused medication. She'd also heard that he was working on some new treatment for autism that straddled the ethical line endorsed by the American Medical Association. Was that what they had been discussing in hushed voices?

She slipped past them into Connie's office, pasting on a brave smile for the twenty-five-year-old brunette. Tom had treated her for depression. Newly divorced with a three-year-old, Connie had been desperate for a job when Tom hired her.

Connie's green eyes reflected remorse. She'd made great strides since starting therapy and taking the job.

Hopefully Tom's death wouldn't cause her to have a setback.

"Hi, Mrs. Wells." Connie's voice quivered with emotions.

"Hi, how are you doing?" Megan's nursing instincts kicked in.

Connie's thin shoulders lifted slightly. "Hanging in there. But I sure do miss Dr. T."

Megan smiled, surprised to hear Connie refer to him that way.

"I know he's actually been gone for weeks, but all that time—" Her voice broke, and she grabbed a tissue from the box on her desk, dabbed at her eyes and swallowed, "...all that time I prayed they'd find him alive."

"I know, honey. So did I." She squeezed Connie's shoulder. "But we'll get through this. Just keep telling yourself you have a job now. You have to stay tough for your family."

Connie nodded. "You're about the bravest lady I know, Mrs. Wells."

"I've told you a dozen times to call me Megan. And you don't give yourself enough credit—you were brave to leave your husband, and you're raising your son on your own. That takes courage."

Connie nodded again, seeming to draw strength from Megan's words. Megan brushed at her khakis. "I came to clean out Tom's office, and to take his personal things home." Megan closed her hand around the doorknob to Tom's office, but Connie stood, waving a hand.

"You won't believe this, but they've already brought in a replacement for Tom."

Megan had already pushed the door open though.

She paused, stunned, when she saw Cole Hunter sitting behind her husband's long polished desk.

COLE FELT AS IF DÉJÀ VU had struck him the minute he spotted Megan standing in the doorway. Impossible.

Jones had told him he had never been in Tom's office or met Megan before. So, how could he have déjà vu?

"I...I didn't realize you were going to be here," Megan said.

Cole's stomach clenched. "I didn't, either." He stood, ready to apologize. "Jones said they'd planned to put me in a cubicle, but since..." He let the sentence trail off when he saw the horrible meaning register in Megan's eyes. *No sense wasting good office space, Jones had said.* But he didn't tell her that part. That he had thought Jones seemed cold, impersonal. Then again, sometimes scientists were cold and impersonal. They had to be.

Another little tidbit, he realized, wondering if these small flashes of insight were memories prying through the empty spaces in his mind.

She squared her shoulders. "I came to get his personal things."

Cole's gaze strayed to the photo of her and her husband.

"You looked very happy," he said, his voice tight.

Emotions skated across her face. A happy memory obviously surfacing. Then sadness. And something else he couldn't quite put his finger on.

"That was in the Keys, right? Your honeymoon?"

Her gaze flew to his. "How...how did you know that?"

"I don't know. Maybe someone told me." The image

of Megan in an ankle-length white cotton dress floated through his mind. She'd looked like an angel. Other memories crowded through the haze. A kiss. A long walk on the beach. A sailboat. "The boat tipped and you fell in the water."

His throat grew thick. She was staring at him, a frightened look in her big blue eyes. "Who told you about our honeymoon?"

He had no idea. Worse, just as quickly as the images had come to him, they disappeared. And once again, his mind was an empty hole.

MEGAN GRIPPED THE EDGES of the photograph, searching Cole Hunter's face for some explanation about his comment, but he offered none. Instead he seemed confused, almost as troubled as she was about his knowledge.

She had told only a few of the nurses about their short trip to the Keys. As far as she knew, Tom had told no one. Of course, anyone who had come in his office might have asked about the photo, so Tom might have explained the picture. He certainly wouldn't have shared any details, though.

Tom was not that kind of man.

He kept his personal life and feelings to himself, his business life almost a different entity. If she hadn't worked at the center herself, she might never have met his colleagues.

"I'll step outside while you go through things," Cole offered.

Megan nodded, needing some space. Not only did she dread the task ahead, but being in close proximity to Cole Hunter unnerved her. His presence seemed to take up all the space in the office, filling it with a different sense, a huge, breathtaking masculine one.

A frightening one.

Or maybe it wasn't him at all, but just the fact that he'd been sitting in her late husband's chair.

He reached for the cane and leaned on it, then moved to the door, hesitating. "I'm sorry if my being here makes it more difficult for you."

Megan clamped down on her lip with her teeth. "It's not your fault."

He gripped the door, confusion in his eyes again. "I didn't ask for Tom's office, Megan. Dr. Jones insisted. In fact…"

"Yes?"

"I feel uncomfortable being here, too."

Megan's anxiety lifted slightly. She understood how difficult it was to be the new man on the block. As a nurse and employee of CIRP, she should be welcoming him, easing his transition.

"I do need to review his files at some point," Cole said.

"All right." Megan placed the photograph in the box. "Will you be taking over his patients also? And his research?"

He glanced down at his hand as if her question disturbed him. "Not right away. I recently had an accident myself."

"I'm sorry. Was it serious?" Megan remembered the scars.

"Yes. I haven't fully recovered." She waited for further explanation but he didn't elaborate. In fact, she sensed the accident was difficult for him to discuss. She understood about not sharing one's problems, too; her entire life had been a hard road, one that had kept throwing her curves when she least expected it.

Just as it was doing now.

Cole stepped into Connie's office, wondering where the brunette had disappeared to. He felt a small headache pulsing behind his eyes. He poured himself a cup of coffee from the corner table and massaged the side of his temple. What had happened back in Wells's office? How had he known where the photo of Megan and her husband had been taken? Had one of the other doctors told him? According to Jones, he had only met Tom Wells for a brief minute or two when he'd interviewed for the job. Would he have shared something personal with a stranger? Most men didn't.

"Dr. Hunter, are you all right?"

He pivoted, sloshing hot coffee on his hand.

"Oh, my goodness." Connie grabbed a napkin and wiped at his shirt. "I didn't mean to startle you."

"Not your fault. " Cole had said the same thing to Megan. "I have a headache, that's all."

"Can I get you some aspirin?"

He had no idea why the young woman was so jittery. Was she nervous around all men? "I guess it's just the stress of a new place."

"I know what you mean. I was a wreck when I first came here."

A smile twitched at his lips.

"That must seem weird since I'm acting so nervous now, but I really was a mess. Dr. Wells and his wife have helped me immensely."

He narrowed his eyes, not quite comprehending.

"I figured Dr. Jones told you. He doesn't like me very much."

"Why do you say that?"

"I don't know. Maybe because I was a patient. Dr. Wells helped me with my depression. And his wife, Megan, she's a real doll, so kind and understanding. Anyway, Dr. Jones wasn't thrilled when I took the job here. I guess he thought the center shouldn't hire former patients. He probably thinks I'm not very stable." She blushed as if she realized she'd been rambling.

He nodded sympathetically.

"If you want someone to show you around, ask Megan. She knows everyone in the psych ward. All the doctors, I mean."

"That's not a bad idea," he said. As soon as the words left his mouth, the hair at the back of his neck prickled. Before he even glanced sideways, he knew Megan Wells stood in the doorway. He smelled her body spray, a very soft hint of jasmine, the kind of fragrance she always wore to work. Subtle but fresh. She hated heavy perfumes; too many of the patients had allergies and reactions.

His heart stopped beating. How in the world had he known that?

"WHAT'S GOING ON?" Megan stiffened. Connie and Cole Hunter were staring at her as if she'd interrupted some private conversation.

"Nothing," Connie said with a smile. "I was just bragging to Dr. Hunter that if he needed someone to show him around and introduce him to the staff, that you were the one to do it."

Megan shook her head at Connie's exuberance. Sometimes she acted seventeen instead of twenty-five.

Cole's potent masculinity probably intimidated her. Her husband had been a big man.

*Now, why would I think that,* she thought irritably?

She and Cole were going to be working together. In spite of the circumstances, she had to behave like a professional.

"I'd be glad to introduce you and show you the facilities," Megan offered. "Whenever's convenient for you."

"Thanks. I had a short tour when I was here, and I've met a few people since I arrived, but I'm still not familiar with the layout of the center." He gestured to the door. "Shall we go now?"

"Certainly." She left the small box of items in Connie's office. "Follow me."

She wound through the maze of offices, pointing out the various names of the doctors and scientists and noting each one's specialty. Just being here brought back so many memories of Tom. Maybe she should transfer.

Most of the doors remained closed, and she didn't want to disturb the doctors' work by going inside. Cole would have to meet them one by one as the situation called for or at one of the weekly staff meetings.

"Where are the labs?" Cole asked.

"On the second floor." Megan paced herself to suit his pained gait as she led him through the hospital. The next hour she showed him the various floors and departments, pausing to introduce him to different nurses and counselors.

"Two doctors on this floor are researching a new drug to treat manic depression," she pointed out. "And Dr. Hornsby's pet project is dissociative identity disorder."

"Tell me about the psychiatric ward," Cole said as they entered the wing for the mental patients.

"We see a variety of patients here, some are outpatient and some are here for long-term treatments and must be confined."

"Are all of the patients using research oriented treatments versus traditional therapy?"

Megan shook her head. "Not all. The ones who are have come on a volunteer basis, or they're severe cases where traditional techniques or medications haven't been effective."

They'd reached the main floor of the mental ward where patients were received and assessed. "We have counselors and therapists who assess and interview patients when they first come in. Of course we take referrals from other physicians as well."

"It'll take you a while to get to know everyone," Megan said, sensing he was becoming overwhelmed.

"Ms. Wells," Janie, one of the volunteers called. "Can you come in here a second? Mr. Boyd is asking for you."

"He's been diagnosed with schizophrenia," Megan explained softly to Cole. "But he's been doing so much better with the new medication."

Cole followed her inside the small room. Megan winced when she saw Daryl Boyd hunched into a ball on the floor, his hospital gown gaping. "Mr. Boyd, what's going on?" she said softly, kneeling beside him.

A tuft of thin gray hair spiked haphazardly over his freckled head, his eyebrows were bushy, and his eyes wild. He glanced at Cole and pointed a shaky finger. "Who's that?"

"This is Dr. Hunter," Megan said. "He's—"

''Get him out of here,'' he screeched, ''he's one of them.''

Megan reached out to comfort him, afraid he'd lapsed into one of his exhaustive states. ''One of who?''

''The bad doctors,'' the old man said in a high-pitched voice. He rocked himself back and forth, hugging his arms around bony legs. ''You don't know what they do in here. I do.'' Panic rose in his shrill voice. ''Get him out of here. Make him go.''

Megan frowned. She needed to calm Boyd. ''Mr. Boyd, Dr. Hunter is new on the staff—''

''No, I've seen him before. He does bad, bad things. Make him leave!''

Megan stroked his back while April ran in with an injection. Cole arched an eyebrow as if to ask if he should help, but Megan gestured for him to leave. As soon as he stepped from the room, Daryl Boyd broke down and began to cry.

''What happened?'' April asked.

''He was asking for me,'' Megan explained. ''When I came in, he was agitated.''

''They hurt people, they—'' the old man began to hum ''—they hook you up to these wires and put this helmet on you and fry you. My head, it sizzled, it—'' he grabbed his head, covered his ears and rocked faster ''—I thought it was going to explode.''

''Listen, Daryl—''

''You got to be careful, Ms. Megan.'' Boyd dropped his head forward like a child, emitting a low screech. ''Don't tell 'em I told you, don't tell 'em,'' he whispered. ''Or they'll kill both of us.''

# Chapter Four

Cole stood in the hall, watching the hustle and bustle of the staff, troubled by the patient's response to him. Schizophrenics often lapsed into delusional behavior, he reminded himself, so he shouldn't be so disturbed that the man had accused him of doing disreputable things.

There was no way Daryl Boyd had ever seen him before.

The fact that he had a new face was proof of that.

But had he confused him with someone else?

He had heard about the trouble at the center a few weeks ago, that the CEO Arnold Hughes had disappeared and was thought dead, although some speculated that he might have escaped the explosion on his boat. That Hughes might return to Nighthawk Island to run the company or that he was still running it via some kind of secret mode of communication. Police suspected some questionable techniques were being tried at the center, and Nighthawk Island, with its special security and isolation was being scrutinized.

There couldn't be any truth to the things the delusional Boyd had said, could there?

Why had Cole chosen to leave his old job and join the center with the negative publicity surrounding it?

Maybe because he believed in the research and development of the area; the doctors were doing revolutionary things and he wanted to be a part of it. Maybe because he'd believed all the trouble at the center had ended with Santenelli's death.

Even as he rationalized the answer, it didn't feel right.

Perhaps something had happened back at Oakland that had prompted him to transfer.

Megan Wells stepped into the hallway, looking calm in spite of the horrific wailing echoing from the confines of the room. "He'll be okay in a few minutes, once the sedative takes effect. April's going to stay with him until he goes to sleep."

Cole nodded. "Does he have those episodes often?"

"No, that's what's so troubling." Megan wrinkled her nose. "He's usually very friendly with the staff. I've never seen him get so agitated with a doctor before."

"Was he under your husband's care?"

"Yes, but Dr. Jones is treating him now." Megan folded her arms across her waist. "Boyd had been responding to this new drug. Hopefully Dr. Jones can adjust the dosage and stabilize him."

"Right."

"Are you going to be taking on patients right away?"

Cole's hands tightened by his side. "No, not for a while. I need some time to acclimate. Review charts."

Besides, how could he help others when he couldn't sort out his own life?

"What's your specialty, Dr. Hunter?"

"I…" he struggled to remember when the answer

suddenly came to him. "Dissociative identity disorder. I was working on hypnosis techniques to help traumatized patients regain repressed memories."

Megan's gaze locked with his, her blue eyes sparkling in the glare of the hospital lights. His groin tightened, and the strong pull of sexual awareness thrummed through him. But he ignored the simmering attraction as research data on the disorder flashed through his head. The latest cases identified in the States. The patients here who were under Wells's care.

Had he read about them or was it a memory surfacing?

"I should have known," Megan said interrupting his thoughts.

"What? I mean why?"

"Because that was one of Tom's areas. I suppose that's the reason you were brought in to work with him."

Cole nodded. "I'll be looking over his files this week."

April emerged from inside the room, thumbing her fingers through her bangs. "He's finally resting. Did something happen to trigger his episode?"

Megan shrugged. "Not that I know of. He did get more agitated when Dr. Hunter came in, but he was upset before then."

April introduced herself. She was attractive, Cole noticed, tall and slender with a heart-shaped face and almond colored eyes. Although she didn't have the same gut-wrenching effect Megan Wells had on him.

Too bad; she was much more attainable than a woman who'd just been widowed.

Irritation hit him. How could he think about a flirtatious relationship with anyone, much less a dead man's wife, when his life was in such turmoil?

For a brief second, April sized him up, a flicker of approval in her smile. "It's nice to have you on board, Dr. Hunter. If you need help learning your way around, feel free to ask."

"Actually, Me… Mrs. Wells has been giving me the tour."

April's smile seemed tight. So she had been interested.

"All right." April brushed his hand with long nimble fingers. "I'd be glad to brief you on anything else you need."

"Daryl mentioned something about patients being hooked up to electrodes," Megan said, seemingly oblivious to the tension between him and her friend. "It sounded like shock treatment. April, do you know of anyone using that technique now?"

April shook her head, removing her plastic gloves. "But I wouldn't go around asking questions, Meg." Her voice grew low. "You know how sensitive some of the scientists and doctors are about their work, especially the classified projects. If I were you, I'd just keep my mouth shut and do my job."

APRIL'S WARNING BUGGED Megan as she walked Hunter back to his office. She certainly understood privileged information, confidential cases, and the importance of not divulging the research center's confidential work, but in light of Tom's death and this new man's presence, curiosity ate at her. The timing of everything—Arnold Hughes's disappearance, Tom's death, Cole Hunter's appearance and now Daryl Boyd's claims about strange things happening at the center seemed way too coincidental.

"Thanks for the tour," Cole said when they reached Tom's office. Now Cole's.

"Certainly." Megan tried to ignore the subtle tension between her and this man. It had been eons since she'd felt this magnetism. Maybe never.

Guilt suffused her for the thought. Just what had attracted her to Tom?

The fact that he'd been safe. That he'd offered security, someone to lean on, when she'd never known any. She noticed a stack of mail on one of his bookshelves, a card on top. She picked it up without thinking, her eyes tearing when she noticed her name scribbled on the envelope. Tom had bought it for her but hadn't given in to her.

"What's that?" Cole asked.

"A card from Tom." She opened the envelope and removed the card, smiling at the yellow daises on the cover. Daisies were her favorite flower. Inside, she skimmed the few words he'd written, *Dear Meg. I know things have been rocky, but I still do love you.*

Why hadn't he given her the card?

She brushed a tear away, faintly aware Cole was watching her. Before she realized what had happened, he stroked her arm.

Megan jumped back, amazed at the tingle that spread through her at his touch.

"I'm sorry." An odd look darkened his eyes as if he'd felt the same electric charge pass between them. Several tense seconds lapsed before he spoke again. He indicated a folder in his hands. "Did you know what your husband was working on?"

Megan startled, remembering how secretive Tom had been the last few weeks she'd seen him. "Not exactly. He pretty much kept his work to himself."

But she wanted to know, she thought, a firm resolve setting in. She wanted to know that he hadn't been involved in anything illegal or unethical. That he had loved her and that he had died in an accident. That if he had lived, they could have worked things out.

Then she could put the questions in her mind to rest. And maybe she could move on with her life without so many misgivings.

COLE SPENT THE AFTERNOON poring over the case files he'd inherited from Tom Wells.

Amazing, but Wells's notes on hypnosis seemed familiar.

As did the details and information on three of his patients. Harry Fontaine. Frank Carson. Jesse Aiken.

Just as Wells's wife Megan felt familiar.

He'd had another flash of an image when he'd touched her earlier today. Before he'd seen her open the card, he had known it had daisies on the front.

But how could he know that? And how could he recognize those files if he'd never read them or met the patients?

Impossible.

Unless he had spoken with Wells on the phone about them? Perhaps they'd consulted since they'd been studying similar areas of work. Maybe he should use some of the hypnotic treatments to try and regain his own memory. He'd have to speak to his doctor about it.

And maybe Wells had told him about Megan. That she liked daisies.

But he doubted it.

Remembering the questions he'd had about his work back in Oakland, he searched the Rolodex, listing the companies affiliated with CIRP until he found a listing for Dr. Frank Chadburn, director of the psychiatric department at Oakland.

He punched in the number. Maybe Chadburn could shed some light on Cole's life and fill in some of the details about his move to Savannah.

"I DIDN'T THINK YOU WERE working today." April poked her head into the file room.

Megan glanced up from the folders in her lap, hoping guilt didn't show on her face. She'd been scanning the charts for anything that might support Daryl Boyd's allegations. April would simply say the man was delusional, which she knew true to an extent, but still, the timing of Tom's death with Cole's Hunter's appearance, and the patient's rantings bothered her. She had heard of a shock treatment similar to the one he'd described that had been used at another facility, but it had been banned. She didn't know of anyone here who would try to implement it. But she had to know for sure.

Thankfully, she hadn't found anything suspicious.

"I couldn't face going home yet, thought I'd clean up the files."

April frowned. "I know it's tough, Meg. But you can't stay here around the clock."

Megan stuffed the folders back into place. "It's just that the house is so quiet, April. Not that Tom was there that much before, but…but at least I knew he was coming home.'' Even though they'd been separated, it hadn't seemed final.

Not like death.

April leaned over and gave her a hug. ''I know, honey. But it'll get better. In time.''

Megan stood, her legs and back aching from bending over to reach the lower drawers. ''I guess I'll head home now.''

''You want to grab dinner?'' April asked.

Megan shook her head. ''I still have a dozen casseroles at home. Besides, I'm not even hungry. But if you want to stop by, I'll heat one up.''

April shrugged. ''Actually I'll take a rain check. I may have a date later tonight myself.''

Megan arched a brow. ''A keeper, I hope.''

April laughed. ''Maybe.''

''So who is the lucky guy?''

''I'd rather not say, Meg. I don't want to jinx it just yet.''

Curiosity niggled at Megan. ''Someone from the center?''

April winked. ''Now, that's all I'm going to tell you.''

Megan laughed, fighting irritation. Although she considered the woman her best friend, April could sometimes be secretive.

Just like Tom had been.

She grabbed her purse, ready to leave. Tonight she'd sort through his things, maybe see if she could access his files. And maybe she'd figure out what he'd been hiding from her.

''DR. CHADBURN, THIS IS COLE Hunter.''

''Yes, how are you doing?''

Cole's fingers tightened around the phone as he focused on the man's voice. He didn't recognize it. "I'm settling in. I suppose you heard about my accident."

"Yes, so sorry, son. You were on your way to Savannah when it happened."

"So I've been told. My memory's pretty foggy, though."

"Ah, I see. Well, what can I do for you?"

Cole leaned back in the swivel desk chair and massaged his temple, fighting another headache. "I'm trying to talk to people and see if it jogs my memory. Can you tell me the circumstances surrounding my transfer from Oakland."

A moment of hesitation followed. Finally Chadburn cleared his throat. "I'm not sure what you mean, except that you'd been in touch with the research center there for months. The facility is much larger, with more cutting edge techniques for treating psychotic disorders. It seemed a natural fit."

Cole frowned. So it had been a smooth transition.

Then why did he have this nagging feeling that just before his accident he'd been arguing with one of the doctors? Trouble was, he didn't know if it had been someone from Oakland or CIRP. And he had no idea what they might have argued about.

"I JUST RECEIVED A CALL from Frank Chadburn at Oakland. Cole Hunter called him."

He yanked his cigarette pack from his pocket and tore open the cellophane. "Damn. What did he want?"

"Chadburn said he wanted to know the conditions of his transfer here. Chadburn stuck to the story we'd worked out."

"Thank God. You think he suspects something?"

"I don't know. Hunter claimed he was just trying to jog his memories by talking to people he knew."

He lit the cigarette, inhaled, tried to calm himself.

"Just keep a handle on the situation. Spend some time with Hunter, make him focus on work. That's the only reason he's here, you know."

"Right."

"And Wells's wife?"

"I'm watching her as well." A job he didn't mind at all.

But he didn't like the fact that Hunter had spent the morning with her. Or that he was asking questions. And if he got anywhere near the truth, if he went searching for information about the real Cole Hunter, he'd have to do something to stop him.

MEGAN STOPPED BY CONNIE'S office to pick up the box of items she'd packed earlier.

"You heading home?" Connie asked.

"Yes. How about you? Don't you need to pick up your son from day care?"

Connie flicked off her computer. "Yeah. After I check on Dr. Hunter, I'll hit the road."

"You want me to wait so we can walk out together?"

"No, go ahead. He might need something. You look worn-out, Megan."

"I am. Give little Donny a hug for me."

Taking a last look at the closed door where her husband used to sit, Megan clutched the box in her hands and left. But she couldn't squelch the questions tumbling through her head as she walked down the hall to the lower parking deck. Why did Cole Hunter rattle her so?

The sun was beginning to fade, and the early evening shadows in the garage played havoc with her nerves. Last night she had thought someone had come into her house. Had she been dreaming? Had she somehow opened her window without remembering it or had someone really been there? And if so, who? And why?

Hurrying now, she fumbled with her keys, checking the parking lot for other workers. Odd that the place was nearly deserted when it was only a little past five. Of course, the evening shift had just come on the hospital at three, so she had missed the daily changeover. A footstep sounded behind her and she scanned the area behind her, but saw nothing. The whisper of cigarette smoke drifted toward her.

Her pulse racing, she finally unlocked her SUV and slipped inside. Still scanning the dark spaces of the garage, she locked the car door, then carefully placed the box onto the floor, and started the engine. Heart racing, she threw the car into gear and sped out of the lot. A pair of headlights nearly blinded her as she pulled onto the street. The car swerved and honked at her, then raced on. Megan exhaled a shaky breath and forced herself to lift her foot from the accelerator. She was fine. Safe.

For heaven's sakes, if she didn't stop this, she was going to need therapy herself.

Music usually relaxed her, so she switched on the radio and turned onto the highway toward Savannah. The bay bridge loomed ahead and she fell into traffic. A strange odor permeated the car, though. She sniffed, trying to put her finger on the scent, but she couldn't figure out the source. She glanced around the vehicle for a damp towel or bag of trash that might be causing the foul smell, but saw nothing. The traffic slowly eased over the bridge, the pace picking up as some of the cars turned toward Whistlestop Island.

A small white puff of smoke drifted up in front of her. It took Megan several seconds to realize the smoke was coming from her vehicle. The engine was on fire.

She tried to remain calm as red-hot sparks spewed from the hood. It must have overheated. She'd pull over and let it cool. Call a mechanic.

She swung the Explorer to the side of the road, bouncing as it hit the rocks along the coastal line, then stopped just before going over the embankment. Her heart racing, she jumped out of the car. A second later, the entire vehicle burst into flames.

# Chapter Five

Cole rubbed at his neck as he maneuvered over the bay bridge, his gaze straying to the envelope holding Tom Wells's appointment book which he'd jammed in between the console and seat and passenger side. He'd found it as soon as Megan had left and had tried to catch her, but he'd missed her, so he decided to drop it by her place. He'd also discovered a silver compact in the desk drawer. Assuming it was hers, he'd brought it as well.

The thick evening traffic slowed, the sight of smoke drawing his eye in the fading sunset. He watched a flume of smoke curl into the graying sky, flames shooting upward in jagged orange and red lines. His chest caught when he realized the burning wreckage was a Ford Explorer. The same one Megan Wells drove. Was she inside?

He steered off to the left side of the road and drove along the embankment. Finally he spotted her standing a few feet from the burning wreckage.

Thank God.

But what had happened?

Hunched over, with her arms wrapped around herself

as if she might collapse, she looked dazed and confused. And so damn vulnerable, a surge of protectiveness swept over him.

His heart pounding, he swerved off the road and screeched to a stop. He threw open the door, grabbed the cane, then limped toward her, cursing his weak leg.

MEGAN'S SHOCKED GAZE was glued to the site of flames consuming her SUV. A man in a black pickup had stopped and phoned 911, two other cars had joined him.

"Ma'am, are you hurt?" one of the bystanders asked.

"Did you get burned?" the elderly woman with him asked.

"No. I...I'm fine." In spite of the heat, Megan's teeth chattered. If she hadn't gotten out when she had, she would be trapped inside.

And most likely dead.

"Megan!" Cole Hunter suddenly appeared beside her, winded and looking concerned. He gently grabbed her and turned her toward him. "Are you all right?"

Megan nodded, hating the sting of tears pricking at her eyes.

"What happened? Did someone hit you?" He checked the area, searching for another car, but the ones that had stopped were apparently innocent onlookers who'd tried to help.

"No, I smelled a weird odor, then I saw this puff of smoke—" Her voice broke, but she inhaled to gain control. "So I pulled over, but when I got out, the whole car burst into flames."

Megan swayed. Cole pulled her into his arms, holding her tightly as they waited on the emergency vehicles. A police siren wailed in the distance, and the sound of a fire engine roaring toward them drowned out the sound of the waves lapping at the shore. Heat scalded them, the crackling of burning metal splintering through the silence.

Seconds later, chaos erupted as firemen roared to a stop, jumped down issuing orders, and began trying to hose down the flames. One police officer instructed by-standers to move along and began to direct traffic, while the other one introduced himself as Wayne Lamont. "Ma'am, what happened here?"

Megan tried to pull herself together and reiterated the same story she'd told Cole Hunter.

"So no one else was involved?" the burly officer asked.

"No."

Lamont wiped sweat from his face. "Did you hit something, run off the road, lose control?

"No." Megan mentally replayed those last few seconds. "I just smelled something odd, wasn't sure what it was, then I saw smoke so I figured the engine had overheated." The flames were dying down with the on-slaught of water from the fire hose. "When I stopped to check the engine, the whole car burst into flames."

"Did you check your engine gage before you got out?"

Megan frowned. "Yes, when I first noticed the smell, but it was normal."

"It wasn't registering hot?"

"No. What would make it do this?"

The policeman pulled at his double chin. "I don't know, ma'am. Faulty engine or a gas leak maybe. We'll check it out."

"You do that," Hunter said in a strained voice. "Make sure there's no foul play."

The cop raised a thick gray eyebrow. "What makes you think it might be foul play, mister?"

Megan glanced at Cole wondering the same thing.

"Cars just don't catch on fire," Cole said, a dark look in his eyes.

"Can I get your name, sir?"

"Cole Hunter. A…a friend of Ms. Wells."

A friend? She barely knew this man. And how had he arrived so soon after the fire?

Shadows darkened his eyes as he gazed at her. Had he read her mind?

"You really think the fire might not have been accidental?"

"Yes."

But why would he suspect foul play? And why had he shown up when he had?

"I'm just trying to protect you, Megan."

She remembered the questions she'd had about Tom's death, Cole's sudden appearance, the unsettling feeling that someone had been in her house, Boyd's accusations earlier in the day, the whispered warning that she might be in danger in the night. Fear gripped her. What was going on?

"DO YOU NEED A RIDE HOME, Mrs. Wells?" Officer Lamont asked after he'd written down her insurance information. The other policeman questioned the two cars that had stopped, then sent them on their way.

"Thanks, that would be—"

"I'll give her a ride," Cole offered.

Megan opened her mouth to refuse, but he silenced

her with another one of his dark looks. He didn't understand the fierce protective instinct that came over him, but he had to make sure she arrived home safely.

"We work at the same place," Cole explained when the policeman arched both eyebrows. "Besides, I was planing to stop by her apartment anyway. I have some things from the office for her."

Lamont shrugged. "All right with you, ma'am?"

"I suppose." Tension knotted Megan's muscles. If Cole meant her harm, surely he wouldn't announce to the police that he was driving her home.

"Let your insurance know about this right away, Ms. Wells. We'll call you when our report is finished."

Megan nodded and moved as if on autopilot when Cole led her to his Jetta. As soon as he slipped inside the car, the tension escalated.

"Are you sure you're all right, Megan?"

"Yes." She fidgeted with a loose thread on her shirt, then remembered the seat belt and buckled it securely. "Were you really coming by my apartment?"

"Yes." He wove into traffic. "I found some more of your husband's things. I thought you might want them." He indicated the envelope stuck between the console.

Megan lifted the manila envelope, her hands still shaking. He ignored the urge to fold her in his arms and tell her everything would be all right. That he would take care of her.

He had no right. No connection to Megan Wells. And he had to remember it.

Recovering his memory had to take first priority.

She opened the clasp and pulled out her husband's personal appointment book.

"I didn't know if you'd want that, but—" He shrugged. "I thought you might."

She flipped through the book, not really reading the contents, but absorbing the fact that it held Tom's handwriting.

"There's something else, too," he said, gesturing toward the envelope.

She frowned and reached inside, then slowly removed the silver compact. Her eyes narrowed as she turned it over and examined the back etchings.

"Where did you find this?" she asked in a quiet voice.

He cut across the left lane and veered into town. "Tom's desk. I figured you'd left it there sometime—"

"It's not mine."

If it didn't belong to Wells's wife, then whose was it?

The most obvious answer—it belonged to another woman. The same suspicions flared in Megan's eyes.

Was her husband having an affair before he died?

MEGAN TRACED A FINGER OVER the expensive silver compact. Had Tom been involved with someone else? Had another woman captured his heart and given him the happiness she'd been unable to? Was this woman the reason for all his secrets and not his job as she'd thought?

Hurt and anger twisted inside her, carving a hole in her already shattered emotions. "It must belong to Connie," she said finally, stuffing the compact back in the envelope.

He nodded, although she saw a muscle tick in his

jaw. He didn't believe her. Had he known more about Tom than he'd revealed?

She was surprised when he headed toward the section of town where she lived. In fact, he pulled into her driveway without once asking for directions. The beautiful azaleas had turned brown, shading the sun from the front door.

She studied Cole's features. "How did you know where I lived?"

He shrugged, gazing at her with that same intense look. "I...I don't know. Maybe someone told me. Maybe I've been here before."

"You haven't." She glared at him. "How well did you know my husband, Dr. Hunter?"

His jaw tightened. "Not well. What little I did know, I've forgotten."

She laced her hands over the envelope. "What do you mean, you've forgotten?"

Cole raked a hand through his hair, the scar more striking in the glare. "Let's go inside and I'll explain."

"No, why don't you tell me now. You're hiding something and I don't like it."

"I don't mean to be hiding anything."

"What kind of answer is that?"

"I told you I was in an accident." He reached for the door handle, then stopped as if he realized he was frightening her. "I suffered a head trauma in the accident, Megan," he said in a low voice, "and I...I lost my memory."

Megan's breath caught. He sounded sincere, yet should she trust him? "You mean you have amnesia?"

"Yes. I may or may not ever recover the memories.

That's one reason I'm not ready to start seeing patients yet. I may never be."

She unfastened her seat belt ready to escape if need be. "What do you remember?"

"Not much," he admitted. A long-suffering sigh escaped him. "When I read some of the files, I recognize the technical terms. But I don't remember my name, much less anything about my life as Cole Hunter, not where I lived, my family, where I grew up, nothing except for the things Jones and Parnell told me. I don't even remember coming here for an interview or taking this job." He stretched his hands in front of him, rubbing a finger over the puckered scar. "All I know is that I came from Oakland Research Institute in Tennessee. That's where I signed on to work with your husband. And..."

"And what?"

"And..." He hesitated again. His voice turned low, husky. A smoldering heat warmed his eyes as he stared into hers. "And that there's something about you that is familiar, too."

A strained heartbeat passed between them. Megan wet her dry lips with her tongue, forcing herself to take a deep breath. The car closed around her as if it had suddenly shrunk.

"But that's impossible." She hated the quiver in her voice. "We didn't meet until Tom's funeral."

He touched her hand, stroked her fingers one by one, then turned her hand over and traced a heart in the center of her palm. Tears filled her eyes while a bizarre feeling engulfed her. Tom used to do the same thing.

Who was this man and how did he know that Tom had done that?

Panicking, she swung open the car door and nearly fell out. Heart sputtering, she hurried up the steps to her flat, fumbling with the key to the door. The older home had been divided into two apartments; hers occupied the bottom floor. Thankfully the other tenant had his own entrance.

Cole appeared beside her in a flash, yanked the keys from her hand and frowned at her. He'd left the cane in the car. Without it, he seemed even more imposing. Manly. "You don't have to be afraid of me, Megan. I'm not going to hurt you."

A shudder rippled up her spine. "I...I never said I was afraid."

He cupped her chin in his hand, slowly rubbing the pad of his thumb back and forth along her cheek. His eyes darkened to a smoky hue and his breath bathed her cheek in an erotic whisper.

A frightening sense of déjà vu encompassed her.

Then his lips parted and he tilted his head as if he meant to kiss her. Megan froze.

"I won't hurt you, Meg," he said in a husky voice. "You can trust me." He cupped her face in his hands and hunger flashed in his eyes as he lowered his mouth to hers. Megan couldn't move, couldn't force herself to stop him. His mouth brushed hers so gently, butterflies fluttered in her stomach. He closed his lips over hers, and pulled her to him, holding her against his hard body as he sipped at her mouth in a long slow kiss that made her body yearn for more.

A hot surge of need, of desperation tore through Megan at the low moan rumbling from his throat. She answered with one of her own, her heart thumping wildly as his tongue teased her lips apart, as he probed the inner recesses of her mouth with his tongue.

But this was all wrong.

She was a married woman, she could never cheat on Tom, no matter how far apart they had been…but she wasn't married now, a tiny voice whispered. Tom was gone.

Forever lost. As was the chance to try to make their marriage work.

But he had only been gone a few short weeks. And she knew nothing about this man, except that he had unnerved her from the moment she'd met him. His hands raked down her back to pull her closer into his embrace. His chest felt like a band of steel, his shoulders so broad she ached to lean into him. Ached to let him make her feel whole again. To make her forget the harsh way she and Tom had ended their last night together. The hurtful things he'd said…

But she couldn't. She had no right to start something with a stranger.

Summoning every ounce of courage she possessed, she firmly pushed away from him. As he stared into her eyes, heat blazed between them, along with a thousand questions. And a tormenting kind of forbidden lust that shook her to the core.

"I'm sorry, Megan, it just seems like…like we were together before."

Only they hadn't been. "Look, Dr. Hunter, I don't know what you think of me but I would never have cheated on my husband."

"I…I didn't mean it like that." He clawed at his hair. "I…I don't understand it myself, but…I just know I spent time with you before."

"I thought you said you had no memories."

"I don't. Well…some sporadic ones. But I sense this feeling that we were together."

That same uneasiness once again splintered through Megan. On some level, she was afraid of this man. On another, she felt a strong pull to him that she couldn't explain… A strong chemistry that spoke of needs and passion and unleashed hunger.

A pull that terrified her.

The blaze from the car fire rose in her mind to taunt her. The fear. Someone being in her apartment. Cole's sudden appearance. The envelope with the things he'd said he'd found. What if he was lying to her? What if he'd fabricated the story about finding the compact?

Steeling herself against the erotic sensations spiraling through her, she let the fear and anger drive her. "I don't know what kind of game you're playing, Dr. Hunter, hinting that the fire might not be accidental. Giving me things you say were Tom's but weren't, then suggesting we had an affair when we didn't. I've had just about enough for today." She grabbed the keys, opened the door and ran inside, then closed the door behind her.

She only wished she could shut out the feelings that kiss had provoked. And forget that for a moment, she hadn't cared if he had scared her. Or that her husband might be watching from his still warm grave, wondering how she could surrender to such hot passion in another man's arms when he'd said she'd been a cold fish in his.

COLE STOOD ON MEGAN'S PORCH, shadows dawning around the house, his body burning with a need so strong he had to fight not to knock on her door.

But he could not sate his desire for Megan Wells. She was vulnerable. Needy. Still grieving over her dead husband. But terror had swept over him when he'd seen her car on fire. For a minute, he'd thought she might be inside. That she might be dead.

Where had this concern, this desperate fear for her life come from? And this insatiable desire?

Images suddenly bombarded him, just as they had when he'd held her. Images of another time when Megan had readily slipped into his arms. A warm spring day when she'd stripped in the dim light of the evening and they had walked naked into the ocean, laughing and teasing like old lovers. A night when he hadn't needed an invitation to kiss her. When he hadn't seen fear in her eyes, but lust. Even love.

He jerked himself out of the throes of the images, then pressed his hands to the side of his head as an incessant throbbing took hold. What was happening to him? How could he see these things so vividly in his mind when he couldn't remember anything else about his life? When the name Cole Hunter still sounded foreign to his tongue? When his face looked like a stranger's? When Megan swore they had never met?

The blood roared in his ears as he staggered down the porch steps. His leg throbbed and threatened to buckle, the haunting memory of that long hospital stay and the surgery dogging him. Was he hallucinating? Wishing those memories into his mind to fill the empty void that he'd felt when he'd been in so much pain?

His accident had occurred around the time of Tom Wells's death. And he had been scarred so badly he'd needed plastic surgery.

Could the doctors have made some kind of mix-up in identifying him? Could he possibly be Megan's husband, Tom?

# *Chapter Six*

Upset by the fire and the interlude with Cole Hunter, Megan spent the evening cleaning out the bedroom closet, packing away Tom's things.

And forcing herself to face the arduous task of learning to live alone.

Tomorrow she would have to contact her insurance agent. Arrange for a rental car so she could return to work. But tonight…tonight, she had to do something to keep busy so she wouldn't think about the unsettling encounter with Cole Hunter.

Tom's tailored suits went into the box first. After that his starched white shirts, monogrammed handkerchiefs, expensive ties, then his casual slacks and polo shirts. Although she was tempted to donate them to charity, Tom's mother might want to go through them first, so she'd send her everything and let her decide what to do with them.

She lingered over his running shoes and tennis racket, wondering how long it had been since he had used either one. Since he had done anything but bury himself in work.

Not that she had been much better. She'd always

wanted a big dog, a golden retriever, but Tom had been allergic to animals, so she'd relented. She'd given in on a lot of things—her pottery lessons, for one, because he'd thought they were too trivial. And she hadn't even unpacked her collection of angels because he'd called them silly.

Maybe she'd look for a dog this week, one that could keep her company and also alert her if anyone broke in. The memory of the night when she'd suspected someone was in the house made her blood turn to ice. She'd find that box of angels tonight. It was superstitious, but maybe they would protect her. And she'd sign up for pottery lessons, too, as soon as she found a class.

Being a psychiatric nurse and having several counselor friends, she knew how important it was to keep one's self involved in recreational activities, especially in times of stress or grief. She automatically toyed with the plain gold band around her ring finger. Why had she let Tom keep her from doing the things she loved?

Shaking off the troubling thought, she tackled his desk next. Although he kept all of his patient files at the office, he often wrote up comments on his research at home, so various files filled with his typed notes had been jammed into the drawers. She pulled them out, sorting through them by date and title, then labeling them and organizing them into a file box she could store in the attic. According to the notes, he'd conducted several studies on autism, although she saw no notations on shock treatment. Other notes contained information on various mental disorders. The latest data focused on schizophrenics thought to have suffered traumatic incidents before age five. She'd hold on to his papers in case someone at the center needed them.

A folder had been stuffed in between two of the notebooks. She frowned when she saw several hastily written notes about two patients who had experienced adverse reactions to a new research medication Tom had prescribed. Fred Carson and Jesse Aiken. She scanned the contents, surprised more when she noticed Tom had recommended the medication be changed, but someone had overridden his suggestion. Who? And why?

Even worse, three months ago both patients had died.

Being a psychiatric nurse, she should have heard about the patients' deaths. Yet she had never heard either patient's name before. And she'd never heard of the medication they had been taking. Even more suspicious, it appeared as if another name had been there, but it had been erased. Who was the other patient and what had happened to him? Was he still alive?

COLE'S HEAD POUNDED AS HE drove back to his cottage. As soon as he made it inside, he collapsed onto the double bed, the whitewashed walls closing around him, the empty hole inside his head opening up, like a tornado, swirling with memories. He welcomed them, hoping for a clue to his past. Instead dark images bombarded him.

*It was night, nearly twilight, the sounds of the ocean a backdrop to the unnatural quiet. The purr of a boat broke the silence. The whisper of the wind on his cheek, the smell of impending rain, the rumble of thunder in the distance signifying a storm, the ominous feeling of being watched. His senses jumped to alert. The dread in his stomach weighed him down like an anchor, the reality of what he had done pulling at him with guilt.*

*He knew what he had to do. But it was dangerous.*

*He moored the fishing boat and scanned the murky surface of the shore, searching for the man he was supposed to meet.*

*A shadow lurked in the distance, barely visible in the dim light of the quarter moon. The dark image scurried between the swaying boughs of the live oaks and fronds of the palm trees. He tried to distinguish the man's face. Had they discovered what he'd planned to do? Had they come after him to stop him?*

*Hands fisted, his heart racing, he searched the shadows again, ready to climb in the boat and flee. But sounds exploded into the night.*

*A scuffle. A man's loud groan of pain. A gunshot. He had to escape. He grabbed the boat's anchor rope but a bullet pierced his back. He staggered, swayed, tasted blood. Another sharp sting slammed into him. He'd been hit again. This time lower. Pain and panic blinded him as he fell to the sand. Salt water sloshed into his mouth. He stared wide-eyed as a wave rolled toward him. The force dragged him out to sea. To his death.*

*Megan's beautiful face flashed in front of his eyes. The love they had once had.*

*The mistakes he had made.*

*If he died, she would have no one to protect her. He had to fight to stay alive. Paddle. Swim. Forget the pain.*

*Or they would make her pay for his betrayal.*

MEGAN STARED AT THE FILES again. The only answer she could fathom was that the patients hadn't been at the facility on Catcall Island, but at the more distant one on Nighthawk Island. Just what was going on out there? And how had Tom been involved?

His work had always been secretive, to a degree, but

he'd never confided that he had anything to do with the classified projects on the government-owned island.

Were there other things she hadn't known about her husband? She tucked the folder inside the box, making a mental note to cross-check the files at work for anything related.

Remembering Tom's date book, she sat down at the desk and flipped through the pages. Appointment dates with patients and other doctors filled the pages. She compared the dates with the dates of the patients' deaths. The notations had been whited out.

A sliver of apprehension snaked up her spine.

Why had Tom covered them up? Who had he met with then?

Her curiosity aroused, she scanned a few more pages, the listings of the last three months. Several notations had been made; Meeting about M-T. Obviously M-T was a code word for his latest research. But what did it mean?

Did it have anything to do with those patients' deaths?

Or with Tom's?

COLE JERKED AWAKE, DAZED. What had happened? Had he been dreaming? Or had the encounter on the shore been for real?

He stared at the cane, but refused to lean on it anymore. Instead, he limped to the bathroom, and found the mirror, searching for scars to indicate that he might have been shot in the back, but he couldn't tell. His shoulders sported rough patches, scars from the scrapes and burns caused by his car accident.

Dammit, he would confront Parnell and insist he give

him some answers. He reached for the phone, his hands shaking. What if the doctors at the center were involved?

He dropped his hand and headed toward the shower, questions bombarding him. If he was Cole Hunter, why would he have memories of Wells's life? Of his wife?

And why would the center tell him he'd been in an automobile accident if he had been shot? Why tell him he was a man named Cole Hunter if he really was Tom Wells?

Unless they had made a mistake with the identification.

Or unless they hadn't wanted him to know he was Wells?

But what reason would they have to keep his own identity from him? Wells was one of their most valuable employees.

He had supposedly died in a drowning accident. The memory of the waves lapping at his face, of tasting the saltwater as it carried him out to sea, grew stronger. Supposedly Wells's body had been attacked by sharks. In fact, he had been in the water so long, he wasn't even recognizable. Dental records had confirmed his identification.

The throbbing behind his eyes deepened as he struggled for answers. For more memories. He swallowed another pill, hoping to ward off the headache. He'd ask his doctor about the pain today. Maybe they could change his medication. He plugged in his laptop and checked the Oakland center's Web site, hoping to trigger memories of his former life. A few minutes later, he accessed a list of research projects, papers and articles written by the staff. Midway into the list, he discovered an article written by Cole Hunter.

He accessed the article and skimmed the contents, a piece on nervous tics. But the date on the article couldn't be right. It was dated twenty years earlier.

Which meant he had to have been in his late teens when he'd written it. Impossible. Even if he'd been a child genius, he couldn't have mastered a doctorate in psychiatry and written a study like that before he was twenty.

Shock waves rode through him at the implication. He couldn't be Cole Hunter.

Unless his father's name was also Cole Hunter and he had written the article. He raced to the counter where he'd left the file Jones had given him about Cole Hunter and scanned the contents, his stomach knotting when he read his father's name. George Hunter.

Not Cole.

The doctors at the foundation had lied to him.

The images of the shooting played over in his mind, so vivid his stomach clenched. If he wasn't Cole Hunter and the images had been real, had been memories, then Megan might be in danger. And that car fire had probably not been an accident.

He picked up the phone to call to confirm that she was okay. His pulse raced when she didn't answer.

MEGAN TOWEL-DRIED HER HAIR as she hurried toward the jangling telephone, but by the time she reached the phone, it stopped ringing. She glanced at the caller ID Unknown.

Just as well. It was probably a bill collector. Financial issues—another burden she had to deal with. She grabbed a cup of coffee, ready to dry her hair when the phone rang again.

This time it was April. "Morning, Meg. Just thought I'd check in. See if you were coming to work."

Megan settled on the edge of her bed. She had considered staying home since she'd barely slept the night before, but she needed to keep busy. "I thought I would. But I have to pick up a rental car."

"What happened to the Explorer?"

Megan explained about the fire, skimming over the frightening ordeal.

"Oh, my God, are you all right?"

"I'm fine. It did shake me up a little." *Then Cole Hunter kissed me and rattled me even worse.* But she couldn't talk about Cole. Not yet.

"You want me to swing by and give you a lift?" April asked. "Only thing is I have to be at work at seven."

"Thanks, but I'll probably grab a taxi and go by the rental car place first. I'm doing the nine-six shift today." Megan remembered April begging off dinner the night before. "So, tell me about your date?"

"It was great. But I still can't talk about this guy. I don't want to jinx it."

"Okay, but you have to tell me soon. I'm dying to know."

"All right."

"April, I need to ask you something about the center."

"What?"

"Have you ever heard of a project called M-T?"

A second ticked by. "No. Why are you asking?"

"No reason, really. I saw something in Tom's notes

about it when I was cleaning out his desk. I was just curious.''

''Listen, Meg. I wouldn't go snooping and asking questions about classified material. You know how tight they guard those restricted projects.''

''I can't help it, April. Daryl Boyd's comments bugged me. And some of Tom's notes have been whited out.''

''Let it go, Meg.'' April's voice sounded concerned. ''Just accept his death and try to move on with your life.''

''I suppose you're right.'' Megan said goodbye, then hung up. She should let things go.

But questions filled her head.

She fingered one of the soft-sculptured angels she'd unearthed from her collection the night before, wondering at her friend's sudden resistance to talk about a new boyfriend and her reaction to her question about M-T.

Of course, Megan had her own secrets now. She hadn't been able to confide about her reaction to Cole the night before, either. Or the fact that she'd found those mysterious files. The doorbell rang, and she nearly jumped out of her skin. Hot coffee sloshed over the rim of her mug and hit her thigh, scalding it. She winced, dabbing it with her soft cotton robe. Who could be here this time of the morning?

The bell dinged again, as if the visitor was impatient.

Belting the robe tightly around her waist, she rushed to the door. If it was a salesman, she would give him a piece of her mind. ''Who is it?''

''Cole Hunter.''

She closed her eyes and sighed, tensing automatically

at the sound of his husky voice. "Look, Dr. Hunter, I don't think it's a good idea—"

"Please let me in, Megan. It's really important."

"What could be so important that you'd come over here at six-thirty in the morning?"

"I can't tell you through the door." He hesitated, and she imagined him turning to leave. She hoped he would leave. But his voice echoed seconds later, full of determination. "It really is important, Megan. I have to talk to you."

"Then see me at the hospital."

"No, it can't wait." His voice turned low, gruff. "I…I think you may be in danger."

COLE'S HEART HAD RACED the entire way to Megan's, the images of the fire the night before haunting him. The sense that Megan was in trouble escalated with every mile.

Thankfully she was fine. At least for now.

She opened the door partway, left the chain connected and peered through the narrow opening. He drank in the sight of her creamy skin, her golden hair, those sky-blue eyes and steeled himself against reaching for her.

Because it seemed the natural thing to do.

She wouldn't welcome his touch, though. In fact, she looked terrified of him.

"Why would you say something like that?"

He saw the fear, but read anger in her voice, too. Good, he could deal with anger. He was used to dealing with that.

"I'm sorry. I didn't mean to scare you—"

"Well, you are frightening me. Now who are you and why are you threatening me?"

"I'm not threatening you." Cole had to explain.

But how could he when he didn't understand what was going on himself?

"Please just let me come in." He raised his hands in a helpless gesture, hoping to alleviate her fears. "I…we have to talk. It's about Tom."

Her breath hitched out. "What about Tom?"

He indicated her robe, her damp hair. The neighboring apartments. "Let me come in. I'll wait until you dress and then we can talk."

She hesitated, still wary. "How do I know I can trust you?"

He had no idea how to convince her he was telling the truth. "Because I won't hurt you. I swear I'm trying to keep you safe. For…for Tom."

She stared into his eyes for a long second, the tension rippling between them. Finally she relented and opened the door. "I'll be back in a minute." Suddenly conscious of her near-naked state, she gathered her robe tightly at the neck and turned and fled to the back room. Her bedroom.

A place where she and her husband and lain together. A place he could see in his mind. Brass bed. Maroon walls. A dark green comforter. An antique dressing table that she had bought at a flea market after they were married.

He staggered back, holding his head in his hands as he wove his way to the kitchen. Hoping to calm himself, he poured himself a cup of coffee and settled down at her oak table, trying to piece together the images in his mind and decide if they were real.

A box of files had been shoved into the corner. He read the label—Tom's files.

Praying the box might trigger more memories and offer some answers, he pulled it near him and began to sift through it.

SHAKEN TO THE CORE, MEGAN threw on jeans and a pale blue shirt. She wanted answers and fast. Slipping on socks, she padded to the kitchen, shocked to find Cole Hunter pawing through Tom's files.

"What are you doing?"

Cole's surprised gaze swung to hers, emotions glittering in the depths of his brown eyes. "I…I'm sorry."

"Is that the reason you came barging in here? You wanted to snoop through my husband's files?" She glared at him. He'd shed the cane today and looked even more ominous and masculine than before. "I thought you had access to his work files already."

"I…I do some," he said, a guilty edge to his voice. "But I thought you might have found some things I haven't seen."

He was lying. She wasn't sure how she knew, but she did know. And his wild-eyed gaze raised the hair on the back of her neck. "I don't believe you. Now—" she paused, clearing her throat and putting a forceful ring to it "—tell me the truth about what you meant earlier or get out."

He dropped the files and nodded solemnly, cupping the coffee mug with both his big hands. Her gaze was riveted to the brown ceramic mug. It was Tom's favorite. Why had he chosen it?

"I'm waiting."

He nodded again and took a big sip of the coffee. "Will you sit down?" He lowered his voice. "Please."

She paused, reheated her own coffee, scraped back a chair, and sat down facing him.

"I didn't mean to scare you."

"Well, you did. Now, why would you say I'm in danger? And what's all this about Tom? Do you know something about his death?"

His eyes widened. "You think his death wasn't accidental?"

Megan shrugged. "I...well, I wondered. Tom was an excellent swimmer. He knew the coves, the weather, if there was a storm that night, he would have gotten out of the water before it hit."

He seemed to absorb that information. "I...I don't know how to say this, Megan. But—"

"But what?" Her voice took on a shrill note. "Just tell me what you know about my husband."

He waited a tense, long heartbeat, then spoke so calmly that she barely heard him. "I've had some memory flashes lately. Last night."

"What does that have to do with me?"

"The memories are of you, Megan. Of us."

She lost her breath. "What? That's impossible."

"We didn't have an affair?"

"No. I told you that already." Her voice took on a hard edge. "I never cheated on my husband." She pointed to the door, but he didn't budge.

"I'm sorry, Meg. I had to ask." He gripped her arm. "But last night I had a memory of being in a boat. Of landing on the shore. I know this sounds crazy, but the memories were so real."

"What does that have to do with me?"

His words were measured. "I think I may be Tom."

## Chapter Seven

Megan stared at Cole in shock. "What did you say?"

"I think I might be Tom." He hesitated, then reached for her hand but Megan jumped up, nearly knocking the chair over in her haste to get away from him.

"Tom is dead..." Her voice shook as she backed against the wall. "I buried him, you were there, you saw them lower him into the grave—"

"I know. But—"

"No." Her pulse raced. She had to escape from this man. Was he crazy? Who was he and what did he want with her? "I think you'd better leave."

"Just hear me out, Megan."

"Why are you doing this? Why would you come here and tell me something like that?" Her voice rose, anger mingling with fear. "What kind of sick game are you playing?"

"I swear I'm not trying to hurt you or play games." Cole raked a hand through his hair, the scar on his forehead a reminder of his recent accident. "I'm just trying to figure out what's going on."

She gathered her nerves, forcing herself not to react

to the lost look in his eyes. Could he possibly be sincere?

"I told you I had an accident a few weeks ago. At the funeral, I remember having this strange feeling that I'd had my wreck the same day your husband was reported missing. At first I thought I was suffering from survivor guilt or something like that, but now…"

Megan watched him massage his temple, but she remained silent. He sounded coherent, not crazy. "Go on."

"Then when we met, I had this flash. An image that we had been together before." He shook his head slightly. "I had some of the same images yesterday when I brought you home."

"I don't understand."

"I told you I was suffering from head trauma, that I'd lost my memory. And that's true, but occasionally I get these quick flashes."

"You met Tom when you came for an interview. He must have told you some things about me."

"That's what I thought at first." He stood, jamming his hands in his hair again. "After my surgery, the doctors at CIRP told me I was Cole Hunter. They gave me a cottage to live in and said I'd come here to work with Tom. But I don't remember anything about growing up as Cole Hunter."

"You remember growing up as Tom?"

"No." He paced to the bay window, stared out at the small back yard. "But I'm pretty sure I'm not the man they say I am. I checked the Oakland Research Center's Web site, and found an article Cole Hunter had written. It was dated over twenty years ago."

"But—"

"Don't you see, Megan. If I were Cole Hunter, I would have been a teenager when I'd started working with them. You and I both know that's impossible."

"But maybe there's two Cole Hunters, maybe he was your father—"

"No, I checked that, too. On the file Jones gave me, my father's name is listed as George."

"But if the man I buried wasn't Tom, who was he?"

"I don't know." He pinched the bridge of his nose. "All I know is that the memories I do have are of you. I know things about you, about your life here with Tom."

Megan's breath caught.

"You have a brass bed with a dark green comforter. You like Jasmine, and your favorite flowers are daisies. You like daisies because the two of you were in a field of daisies the first time you made love."

A shudder coursed through Megan, the uneasiness intensifying as he continued.

"I had flashbacks last night of going to a cove to meet some man. I...I don't know who it was, but I sensed I was in danger. Then someone shot me."

Megan frowned. "Tom wasn't shot. He—"

"He drowned. And I remember being pulled out to sea, but I was shot first." He cleared his throat. "The report said the man you buried—"

"Tom. It was Tom."

Cole simply stared at her, a muscle ticking in his jaw. "The man you buried had been in the water so long he wasn't recognizable."

Megan swallowed, dread knotting her stomach. Where was his logic heading?

"What if our bodies were somehow mixed up at the hospital? Our records maybe."

"But Tom's body had been in the water for several weeks. Weren't you hospitalized right after your accident?"

His eyebrows drew together in a frown. "Right. Then the records couldn't have been accidentally mixed up because we wouldn't have been admitted at the same time." He angled his head, raised his scarred hand, his voice low when he spoke again. "Which means that if I am Tom, the center knows it and they purposely gave me another identity."

"But you don't look like Tom."

He placed his hands on the sides of his face. "I had plastic surgery. This face isn't even mine."

Megan sank into the chair. The secrets Tom had rose to taunt her. The files she'd found. The nagging feeling she'd had all along that his death hadn't been accidental.

The little things Cole Hunter had said and done that had reminded her of Tom. The way he'd stroked her hand that day. Was he telling the truth?

Could he possibly be her husband?

A part of her wanted to believe that this man was Tom, that some bizarre twist of fate had sent him back to her to give them a second chance. Like one of the angels in her collection that had come to life.

But part of her sensed he wasn't Tom. He had a mysterious aura about him. He was too powerful. Too intense. Too darkly male.

And how could she trust him?

Besides, why would the center do something so horrible to Tom, one of their valuable doctors?

April's warning rang in her head. What if the center had put Cole up to this crazy story to see if she knew anything about Tom's work? Tom could have told someone at the center more about their life together than she'd realized. And what if he knew about her room because he'd been in it the other night?

"YOU WERE IN MY ROOM the other night?"

"No. I've never been in your room. I'm telling you the truth."

"But why in the world would the people at the research center lie to you?" Megan asked, still unconvinced. "If you were Tom, why wouldn't they tell you? Tell us?"

He sighed, frustration clawing at him. He knew this was a shocker to her, but he was just as confused. "I don't know. I was hoping you could tell me."

Megan shook her head, as if the questions were piling up, one on top of the other. He understood the overwhelming feeling.

He glanced at the box of Tom's files. "Do you have any idea what he might have been working on the last few months?"

Again Megan shook her head. "He didn't confide in me about his work. But he had been secretive about it."

Distrust colored her eyes. Had Tom been secretive about the rest of his life, too?

She obviously wasn't ready to divulge the details of her marriage or her problems with him. She probably thought he belonged in the ward with her patients.

Or one of his patients. Tom's.

Her blue eyes pleaded with him to stop this bizarre train of thought. But he couldn't. "Megan, I have to know who I am and figure out what's going on. When I had the flashback last night, I remembered something else.''

She froze, stiffening as his hand brushed hers. "What?"

He clasped her hand in between his, then traced his finger over her palm and drew a heart in the center. She flinched, recognizing the gesture.

But he couldn't sugarcoat the truth. Her life might depend on it. "I sensed you were in danger. That whoever had come after me, whoever killed Tom, is going to come after you next."

He paused, hating the fear in her eyes, but knowing he had to warn her. "Tom was planning on betraying them somehow. They'll kill you if they suspect you know what Tom had planned to do on the night he died.''

"What did he plan to do?" Megan asked.

"I…I don't know. I think he was meeting someone, but I have no idea who."

She clasped her hands together as a bone-chilling coldness settled inside her. "I don't know what to believe. Tom loved his work. He was so dedicated, but…''

He took the chair beside her and pulled her hands into his lap. His were warm, big, strong, comforting.

But she shouldn't be comforted by this man. Not unless he was Tom. And if there was any truth to his bizarre story, Tom had lied to her. Had put her in danger.

Her head swam with questions. With uncertainty and fear.

"But what, Megan?"

"I...I sensed something was wrong the last few weeks. He seemed uptight, even at work. But..."

"But what?"

"But I thought he was troubled because of us." Her voice rasped out. "Because of me."

A frown puckered the skin between his eyes. When he spoke, his voice sounded low. Soothing. "You were having problems?"

She nodded slowly, tears pricking at her eyes. "He had moved out for a while. But we were going to try to work out things." Her gaze rose to meet his. "But if you were Tom, you'd know this."

"It's the amnesia. Most of the time my memory is like a big black hole." He stroked her hands gently. "I want, I need for you to trust me, Megan. Whether or not I am Tom, I'm not going to hurt you. I need your help, though."

She swallowed. Licked her dry lips. Ached for him to make this fear go away.

But she could not lean on this man. Not when she had no idea who he was or if he was telling the truth. But if he was Tom, if there was some chance he had survived and come back to make their marriage work—

"You do want to find out what really happened to your husband, don't you?"

She nodded, biting down on her lip. She had to know the truth. But what if he wanted to steal Tom's work? No, CIRP had brought him here.

"Then help me get into Tom's files. Maybe if I know what he was working on, it'll help me understand what happened. What I'm doing here as Cole Hunter." He squeezed her hands gently. "Maybe then I can figure out who I really am. And why the research center would lie to me about my identity.''

She nodded again, knowing she had to help him, had to go along. Only then would she know if the man she buried was her husband, or if by the grace of God, he had come back to rekindle their love.

And if Tom wasn't alive, she needed to know what had happened to him. And why this stranger made her want to forget her failed marriage and fall into his arms.

Megan didn't completely believe him. Cole couldn't blame her. He didn't quite believe he was her husband, either. But he couldn't fathom any other explanation for the fact that he had memories of being with her. That he knew things about her he wouldn't normally know unless he had been intimate with her.

Like the fact that she had a tiny mole on the inside of her upper thigh.

That image had come unbidden to him when he'd been rubbing her hands. He'd remembered stroking other places as well, secret sensitive places that had his body harden just to think about. Whispery touches that she had loved. Places he ached to touch again.

Yet he had no right.

He shifted, his leg throbbing, and thanked her when she set the box of files in front of him. He rummaged through them, glancing through the typed notes of old research material, taking more time on the recent files.

''Did you already look through this?'' he asked.

''Yes.''

''Did you see anything odd?''

Megan hesitated. ''Actually yes. In one file, I found notes on two of Tom's patients he'd been treating with

an experimental drug. He made notes about adverse reactions and suggested they be taken off the drug.''

"Why did that seem suspicious?''

"Because someone else vetoed his suggestion. That
was odd in itself. Then both patients died. It looked as
if there might have been a third patient, but the information on him had been deleted.''

"Tom always kept thorough notes?''

Megan nodded. "Some of the data has actually been
whited out.''

He arched a brow in question. "That does sound suspicious.''

"There's something else.''

He waited calmly, knowing it was difficult for her to
trust him.

"I don't recall either patients' names or any mention
of them at the research center. I think the experiments
might have been conducted on Nighthawk Island. He
also referenced the project with a code name, M-T.''

"Do you know what that stands for?''

"I have no idea.''

"Then let's go to the center and see what we can find
out.''

"Let me change into my uniform. I'll be ready in a
minute.'' Megan stood and brushed down her shirt.
"You realize they won't like us probing into classified
projects.''

"Yes, I do.'' Cole caught her hand, a shimmer of
electricity shooting through him. Her wary gaze met his.
"Megan, listen, I appreciate your help. And I promise
you, I won't let anything happen to you.''

Megan simply stared at him, an emptiness in her eyes

that tore at him, as if she still questioned his story. But he promised himself he would keep her safe.

Even if it meant staying away from her himself.

HE CRUSHED THE CIGARETTE butt in the empty foam cup, then wrapped his fist around the flimsy silk of her panties and fisted it in his left hand, the other cradling his cell phone to his ear. Birds twittered across the sky and the sun stretched in the corner, rising like a cheerful welcome sign. He felt anything but cheerful. "Hunter's at Megan's house again."

"What the hell is he doing there?"

"I have no idea. But I don't like it. It's barely even daylight."

"You know, they may have some kind of connection. Something we hadn't figured on."

Damn right they hadn't.

"What are they doing?"

He strained to see through the front window, his palms sweating when he saw Cole Hunter sitting at Megan's kitchen table, his hands clasped with hers, their heads bowed close together. "I don't know. Talking, I guess."

Although the situation looked way too intimate to him.

Damn. Memories of last night rolled through his mind. Another evening with another woman. One who'd tried to satisfy his appetite with her own voracious one.

Only she wasn't the woman he wanted.

He crushed the cigarette in an empty coffee cup.

The one he wanted was sitting in her house with another man. A man with a new face and a mind that should be focused on work as it had always been.

A man who should have died but who had miraculously come back to life.

Because they had let him.

A man he would have to kill if he started probing too much into Cole Hunter's life. Or the center's work on Nighthawk Island.

# Chapter Eight

Megan spent the morning doing routine patient care, administering meds, and assessing two incoming patients, one a firemen suffering from post traumatic stress syndrome after a recent explosion at a local state building, the other a possible bipolar disorder. Ready for a coffee break, she slipped into the lounge. April sat at one of the round laminated tables with a coffee and an early lunch, a stack of files piled in front of her.

Megan poured herself a cup of coffee, added sweetener, then took a seat on the loveseat, exhausted. "How's Daryl Boyd?"

April pinched the bridge of her nose. "Quiet. Not very communicative."

"Maybe I'll check on him later."

April nodded, and turned to face her. "So, did you get that rental car, Meg?"

Megan nodded. "Yes."

"Did you take a taxi or what?"

"Actually Dr. Hunter gave me a lift to the rental car office."

April frowned. "I didn't realize he lived near you."

Megan hesitated. Then again, April was her best

friend. They usually discussed everything. She had even confided her marital problems with April a few months back, and April had offered advice. "He doesn't. He came over to ask me some things about Tom's work."

"Oh. What kinds of things?"

"He thought I might know about Tom's latest research projects. You know he's supposed to be taking over Tom's patients. And he was working in a similar area back in Oakland."

"I see." April tore off a bite of her bagel sandwich and nibbled on it. "What did you tell him?"

Was it her imagination or was April asking a lot of questions today? "Nothing. You know Tom didn't discuss his private research with me."

"He took the confidentiality thing seriously, didn't he?"

"Absolutely."

"No wonder you two had problems. Couples should be honest with one another."

Megan didn't comment. April was right, but she had respected Tom's privacy. Maybe too much. Now she wished she had known more. Had asked more, at least about his work.

April swirled the coffee in her cup. "Something about that Dr. Hunter seems off, Meg."

Megan clinched her jaw. "I know. He makes me feel uncomfortable."

"Maybe you should stay away from him," April suggested. "Connie said that he's not taking patients. That he was in some kind of accident and Jonesy—"

Megan chuckled; she couldn't believe April called the prestigious doctor that name. But they both recognized Davis Jones as a player and neither intended to feed his overinflated ego.

"—said he suffered some kind of head trauma." April washed the bagel down with a sip of coffee. "He said Hunter suffered memory loss, that he might never recover to full capacity."

"You're saying he might be…brain damaged?"

April shrugged. "They don't know if he'll remember all of the details about his work, or if he'll ever be able to apply it again. The center plans to bide its time and see."

"That's too bad." Did Hunter know about Dr. Jones's diagnosis? "Did he mention anything else?"

April thumbed a strand of red hair behind her ear, her fingers tapping on top of her files. "That the medication he's on sometimes makes him say crazy things. So, you probably shouldn't believe everything he tells you."

Megan's hands tightened around the coffee cup. "You mean he hallucinates?"

April shrugged. "Sad, but he may need psychotherapy. He may be delusional or suffering from emotional trauma from the accident. Jonesy said that he exhibited signs of paranoia while he was in the hospital."

Megan tried to assimilate that information. It made perfectly good sense. After all, the story he told her had been bizarre.

But she couldn't forget the intimate way he'd touched her, his promise to protect her. Or that he had known things about her and Tom that no one but the two of them could know.

COLE SPENT THE MORNING scrutinizing the files and old notes he found in Tom Wells's office. He sensed something was missing. That some of the files and information had been censored. He also found nothing on the three patients Megan had mentioned.

Occasionally, as he skimmed notes on a certain disorder, he found sections that had holes in them. Files that seemed incomplete. Had someone else already examined the papers and removed things they didn't want him to see?

But why? If they'd brought him here to work, why wouldn't he be privy to all of the information on the projects Wells had worked on?

Notes on Wells's work with autistic patients seemed the most complete. He had detailed the history of treatments from the past as well as other research facilities. Everything from shock treatment, which had been taken to extremes, and had been legally banned two years before when a patient had died in a small hospital in New York, to a program called TEACCH which worked with early intervention techniques and appeared to have miraculous success with children.

A knock dragged him from his thoughts and he looked up to see Connie in the doorway.

"Good morning, Dr. Hunter. I thought I'd check and see if you needed anything."

He needed answers, but somehow he didn't think this innocent woman could help him. Then again, she had worked with Wells. He smiled, trying to put her at ease. "Connie, how much did you know about Tom Wells's work?"

She fiddled with the doorknob. "I usually typed up his notes on patients after a session. Made appointments for him. But he never showed me any of his research notes—he preferred to log them in himself.''

Cole nodded. ''Do you know anything about his studies with hypnosis?''

''Only that he was excited about its possibilities. You may want to look at it.'' She went to the file cabinet, rummaged through and pulled out a folder. When she opened it, a puzzled look covered her face.

''What is it?''

''This is weird.'' Connie thumbed through the pages. ''The information on the experimental drug he ordered is missing.''

''He drugged the patients during hypnosis?''

Connie made a noncommittal gesture. ''The medication was supposed to relax the patient. Some people resist the hypnotic state, so this drug simply helped their subconscious relinquish control so they could accept hypnotic suggestions.''

''What was the name of the drug?''

''Cognate.''

Cole jotted it down. ''Wells was also working on a project called M-T. Do you know anything about that project? Did this drug have something to do with it?''

Connie twisted her mouth in thought. ''I'm not sure. You probably should talk to Dr. Jones and Dr. Parnell. They oversaw all his research projects.''

''Right. Thanks, Connie. I think I'll do that.''

His curiosity piqued, he wondered what other uses Wells and the other doctors had found for this mind-altering drug. Was Cole given something similar while he was in the hospital?

WHAT WAS COLE HUNTER UP TO today? Megan wondered. Had he had found anything in Tom's files to indicate what might have happened to her husband? And to Cole himself? She fought the temptation to go to his office and ask, but the uncertainty of his identity and April's comments disturbed her.

She'd ask a few questions of her own. Right after she dropped in to see Daryl Boyd.

In light of Cole's suspicious, Boyd's barely coherent rantings took on a more ominous feel. She had checked Boyd's file and discovered that at one time he had been a patient in the sister facility on Nighthawk Island, that he had opted for an experimental drug doctors hoped would control his schizophrenia. Notations showed it hadn't worked.

But why would he have gone there instead of here for the treatment?

She didn't understand the placement logic at all. All of the research conducted on Nighthawk Island was highly restrictive, whereas nothing on his chart indicated he'd been involved in anything but a normal treatment program. Except for that one visit.

When she opened his door, she grimaced at the sight of his pale, thin face. Early-afternoon sunlight painted the room with a golden glow, highlighting the dark shadows beneath his eyes. He lay sleeping on his side, turned away from the window. He complained sometimes that the bright light hurt his eyes, but the doctors had found no physical reason for the problem; it was just part of his paranoia. She picked up his chart and studied the nurse's notation. He hadn't been sleeping or eating well, and had obviously lost weight. Not a good sign.

But he seemed to be resting peacefully now, so she

hated to disturb him. Maybe she'd come back later.

She stepped closer to the bed to tuck the blanket around his thin shoulders. Just as she moved to touch it, he grabbed her arm.

"Thank God you came back."

Megan stifled a gasp and tried to remain calm. So far, Daryl Boyd hadn't exhibited dangerous behavior, but with his illness and the combination of medication, she had to be careful. "Yes, Mr. Boyd, I wanted to see how you were doing." She gently tried to extricate her hand, but he gripped it tighter.

"You have to get me out of here."

She had heard this plea before, from several patients. "What's wrong?" she asked softly. "Haven't the nurses been paying enough attention to you?"

His eyes took on a wild-eyed look. "I'm not joking, Nurse. You have to help me."

"We're trying to do that, Mr. Boyd. That's why the doctors have been treating you." She smiled, trying to calm him. "Maybe I could arrange to take you up to the solarium for a while. Or to the game room. You like to play cards, don't you?"

He forced her to lean closer. "No cards. I have to get out of here. Please, you have to help me." His voice grew more agitated.

"I know you want to leave, and if you follow the doctor's orders and work hard in therapy, I'm sure they—"

"You don't understand. They tried to take my mind before." His voice grew higher, almost a shriek. "If you don't help me, they'll kill me."

AFTER CONNIE LEFT, Cole searched Tom's computer files, not surprised to find that he needed a code to access most of his material. He would have to talk to Megan, see if she knew Tom's password, or if he had backup files at home. He did tap into some personal files and discovered Tom had accumulated some sizable debts. He checked further and found he'd received a hefty payment a few weeks before he'd died and had paid off most of the debt. Did Megan know about the transactions? Had Wells received the bonus for going along with unethical practices at the center?

Frustrated and tired, he stood and stretched, then left the office in search of Davis Jones. Maybe the man would have some answers for him. But he'd have to play his cards right…

A few minutes later, he found him in his office. Jones waved him in. "What can I do for you, Dr. Hunter?"

Cole scanned the walls, noting Jones's impressive credentials framed in the center. "I have some questions about Wells's research."

Jones rocked back in his leather chair and steepled his hands. "So, your memories of your work are returning?"

"Slowly." Cole claimed a seat in one of the brown wing chairs facing Jones's desk. "The patient files are familiar, but I'm curious about Wells's project, M-T. I can't find any details on the project, and I haven't been able to access Wells's files."

"That project was scratched. No need to even bother with it. I suggest you focus on remembering your own research regarding hypnosis."

Cole nodded, determined to ask a few other questions while he was here. "After my accident, why was I brought here instead of the main hospital in Savannah?''

Jones didn't miss a beat. "The paramedics who pulled you from the wreckage found a notebook with the center's name in it—you were on your way here for a meeting and had a file in the seat beside you. They phoned Dr. Parnell and he immediately insisted they bring you here." Jones pulled up his appointment book and glanced at it as if he'd just remembered a meeting. "Why all the questions, Hunter?''

"Just curious, I guess." He had to tread lightly. "Maybe I should visit Oakland for a few days, see my old home turf, old office. That might trigger my memories.''

A frown pinched Jones's deep-set eyes. "I don't think you should leave just now. You suffered a terrible trauma. And with the plastic surgery, it's no wonder you've felt disoriented." He extended his palms in a thoughtful gesture. "Take the advice you'd offer your own patients. Give yourself time to heal.''

Cole hesitated. Had he seen a flicker of panic in Jones's eyes when he'd mentioned visiting Oakland?

THE DOOR FLEW OPEN and Megan sighed in relief when Dr. Parnell strode in Daryl Boyd's room. Parnell's thick eyebrows bushed out above his glasses as his gaze landed on the way Boyd was clutching Megan's arm. "Ms. Wells, is there a problem?''

"Uh, no." Megan freed her arm, well aware Daryl Boyd's pale face turned a pasty-white at the sight of the doctor. "Mr. Boyd was telling me he wants to go to the game room later. That is, if you approve a small outing.''

Parnell angled his head sideways to study the patient. "We'll see what we can do. Let me have a talk with him first and I'll let you know."

Megan backed away from the bed, hating the way Daryl Boyd had suddenly retreated back into his shell. It wasn't the first time a patient had accused the doctors of trying to hurt them. One patient last year claimed he'd been attacked by several of the orderlies, then beaten by two doctors. Another had sworn that during surgery to repair his knees, the doctors had implanted sensory devices to track his whereabouts and connect with aliens.

So why did Daryl Boyd's behavior bother her so much? And why did she suspect that he wasn't acting out of paranoia because of his condition, that something else might be triggering his erratic behavior?

COLE HAD HIT A BRICK WALL with Jones. The man obviously didn't intend to tell him anything. Megan seemed to be the only link he had to the truth.

Maybe he could convince her to check the files, check his medical records and hunt for anything suspicious. An odd notation about medication, his blood-type... He froze in the hallway near the nurses' station. He'd get Megan to draw some blood and do a blood test. Results wouldn't ID him 100%, but they could tell if he had the same blood type as Tom Wells.

She was walking down the hallway with her friend, April, when he approached. Her friend gave him a once-over, too, a myriad of questions in her eyes.

He greeted them as they converged at the nurses' station.

"Getting settled in, Dr. Hunter?" April asked.

"Yes, thanks." Cole smiled, hoping to alleviate the tension between them. He gestured toward Megan. "Can we talk for a minute?"

She and April traded odd looks while he waited silently. What had they been discussing in the hallway?

"My shift's over anyway." April rolled her shoulders. "I'll see you later, Meg. Be careful, okay?"

"I will." Megan braced her hands on the nurses' desk. "What is it, Dr. Hunter?"

He leaned closer for privacy. "Did you find out anything today?"

Megan shrugged. "Not really. And you?"

"Nothing concrete. Just a few missing files. I asked Jones about that project, M-T. He said it had been scratched."

Megan angled her head in thought. "That could explain why Tom's notes were incomplete. But why white out the data? Normally he'd keep all the information so he'd have a record of anything that didn't work on a project for future reference."

"Some notes on an experimental drug he used to induce hypnosis were missing, too. Do you know anything about Cognate?"

"Not much. But from the notes I saw the other day, I think it's been tried with Alzheimer's patients to help with memory."

Cole contemplated that information. "I tried to access his files but failed. Do you know Tom's password?"

"No."

"Think about it, Megan. Those files might explain the project. Do you know if Tom had backup disks at home for any of his work?"

"I'm not sure." She tapped her chin in thought.

"Wait. There's one drawer of his desk I haven't cleaned out yet. There might be some things there."

"Can I come over and have a look tonight?"

A frisson of fear lit her eyes but she quickly masked it. "I suppose so."

"Megan, did you know Tom had accrued some heavy debts, that he recently received a bonus and paid them off?"

"No."

He grimaced as disappointment darkened her eyes. Obviously more secrets Tom had kept. "I want you to give me a blood test." She started to speak, but he cut her off. "I realize a simple blood test won't tell us who I am. But if my blood type doesn't match Tom's, then at least we'll know I'm not your husband."

MEGAN'S FINGERS TREMBLED as she tightened the tourniquet around Cole's arm, her gaze studying his bent elbow. Did this arm belong to Tom? Cole was about the same size as her husband had been, a little leaner, but his accident would have accounted for that. Was the coarse brown hair on his head thicker than Tom's had been? Had Tom been graced with strong veins the way this man's arms were?

She should know these things, yet the details seemed blurred now.

His breath bathed her face as he watched her tap the needle and insert it into his arm. She stared at the dark red blood seeping into the tube and wondered how she would feel if she discovered Cole Hunter was Tom.

And how he could know things about her if he wasn't.

She didn't believe in ghosts or reincarnation.

His eyes seemed to be boring into her, his intense look so unsettling she nearly dropped the tourniquet as she snapped the thin rubber tubing off his arm.

"It's going to be all right, Megan," he said in a quiet voice. "I'm sorry for putting you through this. If I'm not Tom…"

Her gaze rose to meet his. "If you're not?"

"If I'm not, I've upset you for nothing. Given you false hope. Dragged you into my problems." He brushed a tendril of hair from her face, the movement so gentle that Megan's breath caught.

"I just want to know the truth." She placed the blood sample in the plastic holder, then wiped his arm with a cotton swab and placed a bandage over the spot.

He rolled down the sleeves of his white dress shirt and buttoned the cuff while she ran the blood test. Her pulse raced as she checked the results.

"AB positive," he said quietly. Their gazes met and locked.

The same blood type as Tom Wells.

MEGAN'S HEART THUNDERED in her chest as she drove home. They didn't know anything for certain, she reminded herself. Only that Cole shared the same blood type as Tom. So did thousands of other people. It proved nothing.

Yet she couldn't escape the uneasy feeling that the test results added more doubt to an already gnawing suspicion that something was very wrong with her husband's death. And with Cole Hunter's appearance.

She'd fled the hospital as soon as she'd seen the results. She couldn't deal with Cole right now. She couldn't look into his eyes and see the uncertainty, the questions, the hope that she might be able to help him unravel the truth.

And she couldn't face the fact that he might be Tom.

Or that if he wasn't, he still looked at her as if he wanted her. That she still wanted him.

If Cole was Tom and he'd been shot, then who had shot him? Why had someone tried to kill him? And why had they buried another man in his place and sent Tom back with a different face and name?

It made no sense.

The secrets he'd kept taunted her. The debts he'd accrued. Had Tom taken money to cover up something illegal at the center?

She checked over her shoulder to change lanes and spotted a dark sedan a few cars back. Was it the same car she'd seen outside her apartment the other night?

Her insides quaking, she sped up and turned off a side road, glancing behind her to see if the car followed, but she didn't spot it. Thank God. Ten minutes later, her stomach still knotted, she parked in the parking lot behind her town house and hurried up the steps. The shadows of the huge oak trees backing the property blocked the last remnants of daylight. She could barely see to fit her key into the lock. Maintenance needed to put up a back light; she'd call them tomorrow. Finally she jammed the key in the door, but the door screeched open on its own. Megan's heart stopped. Someone had been in the apartment. Magazines and books were scattered on the floor, the lamp lay on its side...

She reached inside her purse and grabbed her cell phone.

*Call 911. Don't go inside. Run.*

She spun around to run back to the car when someone

attacked her from behind. The force knocked her down the steps, face first into the grass. Gravel and rocks jabbed her face. Then something slammed against her head. Megan tasted blood and dirt. Then everything went black.

# *Chapter Nine*

Cole had to make sure Megan was all right. The way
she'd torn out of the hospital, he'd worried she might
have an accident. Not wanting to crowd her, he gave
her a few minutes to get home while he retrieved some
files from his office to study that night. Among them,
Tom Well's notes on hypnosis as a treatment for trauma
victims with repressed memories.

Night fell as he drove from the hospital on Catcall
Island along the coast, then through the downtown Savannah streets. Whispers of oncoming winter echoed in
the nearly bare trees and the wind that whistled through
the sea oats. He rolled down the windows and listened,
thinking the old legend about Catcall Island was true—
the sound reminded him of the low mewl of a cat. An
eerie sound that did nothing to calm his already agitated
state.

Echoes of his own uncertainty taunted his mind.

The blood tests proved only one thing, that he shared
the same type as Tom Wells. But so did a million other
people in the U.S. He needed more extensive DNA test-
ing, and if his memory didn't return soon, he would

have it done. Even if he had to leave the confines of CIRP to keep the center from finding out.

The row of town houses that had been converted into duplex apartments shifted into view, and he steered his Jetta into a parking spot along the front. Knowing Megan would probably not welcome the sight of him made his trek up the sidewalk even harder.

Shoulders stiff, Cole rang the doorbell, scanning the front yard and neighboring houses for anything suspicious. Nothing. No answer either. He tried twice more, then peeked inside the front window.

His heart stopped.

Someone had broken into Megan's house. Was she inside? Hurt? Was the intruder still there?

His mind racing, he checked the back drive for her car. Inching slowly around the side of the house, he grimaced when he spotted the white Toyota she'd rented. Should he phone the police or search the house for Megan first?

Then he spotted her lying on the ground.

Dear God.

She lay motionless, facedown, her arms and legs sprawled beside her. The back door stood wide open. The intruder had probably escaped when Megan had arrived, but still he kept one eye on it as he knelt and felt for a pulse. He desperately wanted to turn Megan over, but he had to check for injuries first. A low pulse beat at the base of her throat. Thank heavens.

He wished he had a gun, but he didn't, so he yanked out his cell phone and called 911, quickly reciting the address and explaining the circumstances, then snapped off the phone and gently checked her body for injuries. There weren't any visible broken bones so he gently rolled her over, bracing her neck as he did. Long blond hair spilled over his arm, the flutter of her pale eyelashes giving him hope.

"Megan." His voice broke at the sight of blood on her lip. Furious at whoever had attacked her, he reminded himself to be gentle as he wiped the dirt from her face.

"Megan, honey, wake up. Are you okay?"

She stirred, a low moan escaping her.

Relief poured through him. She might be in pain, but at least she was alive.

He cradled her against him, still keeping one eye on the doorway. She whimpered and lifted her hand toward her head.

He quickly skimmed his hands through her hair, fury gripping him at the knot on the back of her head. "Shh, it's okay," he whispered, stroking her face. Her eyelids fluttered.

A frightened, dazed look darkened the blue irises but she finally focused on him. "You—"

"I just got here, Megan. You were on the ground." Dear God, she didn't think he had hurt her, did she?

She squinted, long fingers pressing against her temple. "Who…was in the house?"

"I don't know. I suspect they've already gone, though."

A siren wailed in the distance, coming closer. Tires squealed as the EMTs peeled to a stop. A tear seeped from her eyelashes, breaking his heart. Megan was in danger because of him.

He just wished to hell he knew why.

MEGAN'S HEAD ACHED AND SO did her body. But she felt a strange sort of security in Cole's arms.

A false sense of security, she told herself, when he gently handed her over to the EMT. Shoulders ramrod straight, Cole spoke to the policeman. What were they were saying? Cole followed the police officer as he searched her house.

"Ma'am, you have a concussion," the paramedic said. "We should take you to the hospital for observation."

"I'm fine, really." Megan pushed his hands away to sit up.

Around twenty-five, the handsome paramedic was obviously determined to do a good job. He gently urged her to lie back down. "Listen, you've had a blow to the head—you can't get up that fast, you might get dizzy."

"I know. I'm a nurse." Megan tried to smile past the bruise on her lip. She'd bitten her tongue when she'd fallen and had a gash, but thankfully didn't need stitches. "I really am okay. And I don't want to go to the hospital. I need to find out what happened here tonight."

Cole suddenly appeared in front of her, overpowering her with his tall presence. "Someone broke in and damn near killed you, Megan. You're not staying here. You should go to the hospital."

"So now you're my doctor?" she snapped, angry at him, but not knowing why. She didn't want him here, didn't want him telling her he was Tom, confusing her when she was already confused and hurting. Making her want the marriage she hadn't had, making her want his strong protective arms around her when no one had ever protected her before.

Not even her husband.

Making her want him even if he wasn't Tom.

A shudder gripped her at the thought.

He stared at her long and hard, his dark eyes commanding and full of emotions she couldn't read.

The policeman broke the tense moment by clearing his throat. The EMT helped Megan sit up. "Who did this?" she asked.

"We don't know, ma'am." He pulled a small notepad from his pocket.

"Officer Duncan here. Did you see anything? Anyone?"

"No, nothing." Megan searched her memory but realized she hadn't had a clue someone had been inside until the door had swung open. "The door was unlocked when I got home. When I realized someone had broken in, I tried to run, but whoever was inside attacked me from behind."

He nodded, smacking his lips. "All right. We'll fingerprint the place and see what we can find. When you feel better, you need to take a look and see if anything's missing."

"I can do that now."

"Megan, you need to rest," Cole said.

She gritted her teeth. "Just help me up."

He lifted her, then placed an arm around her waist, supporting her as they slowly went into the house. Except for the cupboards, which had obviously been pawed through, the kitchen hadn't been disturbed. But the furniture was overturned and papers and magazines lay strewn on the den floor.

Her gaze flew to Tom's desk and she stifled a cry. What few papers that had been left inside now were tossed in disarray. Cole helped her over to the desk. She checked the bottom drawer for files, but found it empty.

"Damn," Cole said.

"Something missing?" Duncan asked behind them.

"I'm not sure," Megan said. "Maybe some of my... some files."

He looked confused. "You oughta check your jewelry, ma'am. That's usually where burglars hit."

Megan nodded, although she and Cole exchanged doubtful looks. Instincts told her the intruder hadn't been looking for her jewelry but for information.

Cole helped her into her bedroom and tears filled her eyes. Her sheets and comforter had been tossed on the floor and slashed into shreds. The vile act seemed way too personal for someone looking for work files. And the collection of angels she had only recently taken out lay on the floor shattered and broken. Something about the sight of her small treasures being damaged brought the reality of the attack closer to home, magnified the danger. Judging from the torn bedding, this was also a crime of passion—but who hated her enough to want to hurt her?

Cole's jaw tightened. "The box of Tom's things... it's gone?"

Megan nodded, battling her emotions as she slowly approached the dresser. Cole stood silently by while she opened her jewelry box. All her jewelry, everything there was intact. She picked up the silver chain Tom had given her, the most expensive thing she owned, other than the cameo that had once belonged to her grandmother.

"The silver chain was your first anniversary present," Cole said quietly.

Megan's legs buckled. Cole caught her. In spite of wanting to resist him, she couldn't. On top of the attack and everything else, his presence, his knowledge of the intimate details of her life was too much.

The policeman grunted. "Any jewelry missing?"

"No, it's all here," she said in a strained voice.

A perplexed look crossed his face. "Hmm. You must have come in before he had time to find it."

Megan and Cole let the comment slide.

"Well, ma'am. Like I said, we'll fingerprint and see what we can come up with. But it'll take a while, probably just a random breaking and entering."

"I doubt it," Cole said.

The officer scratched his chin. "What makes you say that?"

Cole described the freak incident with her car. "Will you check on that, see what the police found out?"

"Sure will." Duncan hitched his pants up a notch. "Meanwhile, you might want to go to the hospital and rest."

"I'm not going to the hospital."

Cole cleared his throat. "She can come home with me."

"What?"

"It's my place or the hospital, Megan."

She glared at him. "I'm going to a hotel."

"Then I'll go with you."

The policeman watched their interplay with interest. "We work together," she offered, uncomfortable with his curious look.

He nodded as if he understood. She tried to pull away from Cole, but a dizzy spell swept over her and she swayed. Cole scooped her in his arms and carried her toward his car.

COLE HAD A BITTER TASTE in his mouth while he drove toward his cottage. He didn't like the frail look on Megan's face or the fact that she had refused to go to the hospital. But most of all, he hated the realization that she might have been attacked because of him and the questions he'd asked. She had finally agreed to go to his place instead of a hotel, though.

He scrubbed a hand over his beard stubble, his finger brushing the small scar at the base of his chin. What had he looked like beneath this face? Who had he been?

Was he Tom Wells, Megan's husband? Had he married her, had he promised to cherish and protect her? Had he taken her to bed and made her feel beautiful and desired? Was that the reason he felt so protective now?

A hard knot formed in his stomach, even as a strong need to hold her seized him.

She rested her head against the back of the seat and closed her eyes, as if by closing her eyes she could block out what was happening to her. She looked small and vulnerable, and he ached to pull her into his arms. But he knew not to push a victim.

He jerked, steering the car toward Catcall Island, wondering where that thought had come from? What other victims had he known? Patients he'd seen suffering from trauma or shock?

A few minutes later, he parked in the cottage's driveway, opened the door and hurried around to help Megan. She was already opening her door and trying to climb out when he reached her.

In spite of her protests, he placed his arm around her waist. "Listen, Megan, I know you don't want my help, but you have a concussion. I don't want you falling and hurting yourself worse."

"I hate being weak," she said in a low voice.

He chuckled. "I know what you mean. After my surgery, it was awful not being able to do for myself. A humbling experience."

Megan nodded against his chest and relaxed slightly. He opened the door and flipped open the light, bathing the interior of the sparsely furnished cottage in soft light.

"CIRP owns this?" Megan asked.

"Yeah, they use it for new employees in transit, and visitors or consultants who come in."

He helped her to the beige leather sofa, his heart aching at the agitation lining her face. She glanced around the room and he tried to see it through her eyes. Barely any furniture. Clean white walls. Two pictures of sea creatures on the walls with a seascape motif border around the room. The room seemed cold and sterile.

He had no personal items here, other than clothes. No photographs of family or friends. No collections or memorabilia. Nothing to indicate anything about the man Cole Hunter.

"How did you know about the silver chain?"

"I...I don't know."

"Do you remember giving it to me?" she asked in a strained voice.

He searched his fuzzy mind, then sat down, cradling his head in his hands. She really thought he might be Tom. "No, not really. But when I saw it, I knew it had been a present."

"What else do you know about me? About Tom?"
Her blue eyes widened with fear. "Do you remember
our wedding? Do you remember that your parents didn't
want us to go through with it, that they tried to talk you
out of marrying me? That they thought I wasn't good
enough for you." Her voice rose, near hysteria. "Do
you remember that we were trying to have a baby? That
I couldn't get pregnant, that you blamed me—"

"Megan, stop it."

Tears streamed down her cheeks now. She raised her
hands and hit him in the chest. "Do you remember
making love to me, then telling me I wasn't satisfying
you?"

God, no. He caught her hands in his when she tried
to cover her face. "Stop it, Megan. I'm sorry." He drew
her into his arms and pressed her head against his chest,
rocking her in his embrace, murmuring soothing words,
a dozen emotions bombarding him. She broke into sobs,
low, soft, and full of pain.

He picked her up and carried her to his bedroom,
pushing down the covers with one hand. She clung to
him when he started to release her.

He realized she simply needed comfort, not anything
sexual, so he lay down beside her and pulled her up
against him, stroking her arm gently and letting her curl
up against his chest. Seconds later, she drifted to sleep.

He lay in the darkness and stared at the ceiling, studying the shadows on the walls as he inhaled her feminine
scent.

He couldn't be Tom Wells, could he? He couldn't
have said those awful things to her and hurt her like
that. And if he, no if Tom, had, why had she continued
to love him? To grieve for him?

He tried to place the memories, but his mind swelled with nothingness. As much as he wanted to believe he was Tom Wells, he instinctively knew he would never have said anything to hurt her. Because there was no way this woman wouldn't satisfy him. She was everything he'd always admired in a woman. Strong. Gutsy. Independent. Smart. Beautiful. Inside and out.

And even as she'd cried in his arms and looked at him in fear, even as he told himself he should walk away from her to protect her, desire thrummed through him.

God help him. No matter who he was beneath this stranger's face, he still wanted her.

MEGAN'S HEAD ACHED as she slowly opened her eyes. Someone was pressing soft, gentle kisses in her hair. Strong arms encircled her, the scent of a man's body infiltrated the room, and a muscular thigh pressed against her hips. For a brief moment, she snuggled into the man's embrace, savoring the featherlight kisses he brushed against her neck.

But the sound of the man's deep, husky voice murmuring her name brought her back to reality.

She opened her eyes, turned in his arms, and saw Cole Hunter lying beside her, his arms cradling her against the hard wall of his chest. Panic set in. What had she done? How had she let herself spend the night with this stranger?

This stranger with Tom's memories and another man's face. This stranger who made her quake with fear and unleashed passion.

This stranger who made her want to forget the pain of her marriage and start all over with him.

COLE PRESSED KISSES ALONG Megan's neck, gently lifting her beautiful hair so he could touch the sensitive skin behind her ear, the secret place she liked to feel his tongue. He knew the spot well. Had laved it before and would do so now until she quivered with longing.

Whispering her name, he rubbed one hand along her arm, pulling her harder into his chest. Desire splintered through him, her feminine scent so intoxicating he felt the world spin beneath him. He wanted her with such a ferocity that he had to remind himself to go slow. To peel away her clothes gently so he could ignite the same burning ache within her that consumed him.

All night, she snuggled into the vee of his thighs. His sex hardened just thinking about her.

That would have to wait.

Wait until he had teased and tormented her with his mouth and tongue.

Suddenly a noise intruded, and her body tensed within his hold. The jangling sound continued, pulling him from the blissful sleep and lull of being so close to Megan.

MEGAN FROZE AT THE SOUND of the phone, slowly trying to disentangle herself from Cole's arms, but he opened his eyes and stared into hers, and a strange connection passed between them.

The phone trilled again and Cole frowned, then eased up and grabbed it. He scratched the scar puckering his skin, a visible reminder of his accident. "Dr. Hunter here."

She slowly sat up, then propped the pillow behind her to ward off the dizziness. Cole's shoulders stiffened.

"Yeah. Uh-huh. Really? All right. Let me know what else you find."

Megan gripped the sheet in her fingers as he hung up and turned to face her. Early-morning sunlight painted his face in gold. The dark stubble on his chin gave him a dangerous sexy appearance, and his strong commanding presence evoked every illicit sexual fantasy she'd ever had, stirring desire and passion and vulnerability in the melting pot that her body became around him.

Thoughts she shouldn't be having under the circumstances. "What was that about?"

"That was Officer Duncan."

"He knows who broke into my house already?"

Cole shook his head, his expression guarded. "No. But he did file the report on your car. It looks like someone tampered with the gas line."

"Then it wasn't an accident?"

"No." His voice sounded grave. "Someone intentionally tried to hurt you, Megan. And my guess is, it's the same person who attacked you last night."

# Chapter Ten

Cole detested the look of fear he'd just put into Megan's eyes, but he had to tell her the truth. She needed to be careful.

She immediately withdrew from him. "I can't believe this is happening. Why would someone want to hurt me?"

"Maybe they think you know something about Tom's death or his work that they don't want exposed."

"But that's just it. I don't know anything."

Cole massaged the tension at the base of her neck. "I know that but they must think differently." He cleared his throat. "Or if I am Tom, maybe they're afraid you've figured that out."

Megan fisted one hand and pressed it to her mouth. "But we still don't know anything for sure."

Cole nodded. "We will, though. I'm going to find out the truth, Megan, if it's the last thing I ever do."

Megan hugged her arms around herself while Cole lumbered to the kitchen. He returned with a cup of coffee for her, placing a sweetener beside it. She stared at the small packet, the little things he'd done like Tom stacking up in her mind.

"I'm going to shower. Then I'll drive you by your place to clean up, and maybe we can think of a way to break into Tom's files." He lifted her chin with his thumb. "Better yet, I'll do that. You can stay here and rest."

"I'm fine. I'm not staying in bed."

"You shouldn't push it, Megan." His voice grew low, gravelly. "I don't want you getting hurt because of me."

"This is about me, and Tom, too. You know that." She ignored his grimace. "I'll try to think of a word or number he might have used as a password."

She struggled to compose herself while Cole left her to shower. She had not fallen apart when her parents had died. Or when Tom had been missing. She had gathered her courage and faced the obstacles ahead.

She could do it now, too.

But she needed to keep her distance, both physically and mentally, from Cole Hunter until she discovered his identity and why he had come to Savannah. And why he disturbed her so much and made her ache for his touch. She envisioned him in the shower, his muscular body rigid and hard as water sluiced over him.

Why did she have this insatiable hunger for him?

Even more disturbing, the hunger he evoked had nothing to do with the fact that he might be her husband. In fact, even if he wasn't, she would be attracted to him.

COLE CLOSED HIS EYES and let the warm spray of water wash away Megan's scent. He wished he could wash away his hunger for her as well.

She was in danger, possibly because of him. He had to protect her.

Protecting her did not mean taking her to his bed.

But the seconds before he'd awakened, he'd been dreaming that he was doing just that. Holding her and loving her and giving her pleasure. And taking his own.

He turned off the hot water and welcomed the cold. He had to get his libido under control. And he had to delve deeper into CIRP to find out the truth about his identity and the threats to Megan.

He climbed out and toweled off, noting the various scars on his leg and chest. What would Megan think if she saw him this way? Would she be appalled at the scars? Would she mind?

Pushing the thoughts aside, he wrapped a towel around his waist and shaved, then opened the medicine cabinet and stared at the medicine bottle holding his prescription. Cogrixa.

He'd forgotten to take the pills last night. Odd, but he'd slept better. It was the first time since his injuries that he hadn't dreamed of darkness and death. The first morning he'd awakened without a headache, too, he realized, as he studied his face in the mirror. Even his eyes looked clearer and less shadowed.

All because of Megan?

Or the medication?

As soon as Megan entered her house, a sense of violation engulfed her. A stranger had been inside her place, had touched her private things.

"I can't go to work today until I clean up this mess."

Cole headed to the phone. "I'll help you. But first

I'm going to arrange for a security system to be installed on your house today.''

Megan nodded, grateful for his help as she began to straighten things.

"It might be a good idea if you got a dog, too. Maybe a big one that could be a watchdog.''

Megan dropped the papers and stared at him in surprise. She had mentioned the same thing to Tom before, but Tom was allergic to dogs. Plus, he'd been bitten as a child by a snappy terrier and had never recovered from it. He'd even developed a slight phobia.

"You think I should get a dog?''

He shrugged. "Sure, why not? Big dogs are great pets, especially if you get a lab or a golden retriever. Statistics prove they scare off some intruders.''

"Y...Tom hated dogs.'' She watched him carefully, gauging his reaction. "I wanted a golden retriever but he refused.''

His gaze met hers, a frown puckering between his brows as the implication of her comment sank in. Tension gathered in the air between them, hanging like a frayed rope on the verge of breaking. He finally pulled his gaze from hers and picked up the telephone.

Megan tried to dismiss the unsettling moment as she gathered the loose papers and placed them on the desk. How could he threaten her sanity and make her feel safe at the same time? She couldn't rely on this man; she wasn't sure she could even trust him.

If he wasn't Tom or this man Cole, then who was he? Could he possibly have a life somewhere else? A lover or a wife and family waiting on him to return to them? Another woman who wanted his strong arms to hold her through the night?

THE INTIMACY OF BEING IN Megan's house while she showered didn't escape Cole.

Neither did the implication that his suggestion for her to get a dog had been so natural he'd thought nothing of it. For the past week, he'd noticed dozens of details pointing to the fact that he might be Tom Wells.

But what if he wasn't?

What if it was only wishful thinking? What if he'd grown so enamored with Megan that he was seeing things that weren't there?

And if he wasn't Wells or Hunter, then who the hell was he?

AS SOON AS THEY REACHED CIRP, Megan and Cole drove to his office.

Connie gave them a curious look but Megan fabricated an excuse about helping him locate some of Tom's files. While Cole booted up the computer, she listed possible key words Tom might have used for his password.

She handed him the list and watched over his shoulder as he keyed in her suggestions. He tried several words related to the psychiatric field, then resorted to more common ones; his birthday, his parent's names, his birthplace. When the first attempts failed, Cole glanced at the last date. "Your anniversary?"

Megan nodded, surprised when the date worked. She hadn't thought Tom would be sentimental enough to use it. They waited anxiously for the information to download, but a few seconds later, hit another stumbling block.

"All the files relating to M-T have been deleted," Cole said. "Jones claimed the project was scratched."

Megan tapped her fingernails on her leg in thought. "I wonder if he had a backup disk somewhere."

She accessed the files listing pharmaceutical orders. A long list spilled onto the screen, but she scrolled down and found the order. Cognate. The notation that it was being used for M-T wasn't there, but she was sure it was the same drug. Or a derivative of it.

"Cognate is a memory altering drug?" Cole asked. "Connie mentioned a discrepancy in another file about that order. Could it be listed under another name?"

Megan cited at least two derivatives. Cogrixon was one of them.

Cole pulled the pill bottle from his briefcase where he'd put it after he'd showered. He'd intended to ask Jones about it, to see if it might have caused his headaches. He held it up for Megan to examine. "That's what they've been giving me."

"To help with your memory loss?" Megan asked.

Cole nodded. "Jones said that it had proved effective with some Alzheimer's patients, that it might improve my memory." He leaned on his hand in thought. "But if it's being used for hypnosis, do you think it's possible that it could alter a person's memory?"

"You mean if it's combined with a posthypnotic suggestion?"

"Exactly."

Megan's chest tightened, following his train of thought. Could the combination of drugs and hypnosis be used to alter someone's entire identity?

Connie poked her head in. "Dr. Parnell called. He said he wants to see you in his office, Dr. Hunter."

"Tell him I'll be right there," Cole said.

Connie glanced at Megan as if she wanted to say something, but clamped down on her lip instead.

"I guess I'd better get to work, too." Megan smiled at Connie. "How's your son?"

"Fine. He's starting soccer practice."

"Great, Connie. Sports can really improve a child's self-esteem." How she had wanted a child of her own.

"He certainly has the energy for it."

Cole closed the file and stood, waiting until Connie left.

Cole caught Megan's arm as she started for the door. "You won't go home today without me."

"Listen, Cole—"

"I mean it, Megan. I want to follow you and make sure you get home safely. The security consultant I called couldn't come out until tomorrow."

She sighed. "All right. I'll let you know before I leave."

Five minutes later, Cole strode toward Parnell's office. The doctor waved him in.

"What can I do for you?" Cole asked.

Parnell thumbed his glasses up on his nose. "How's the memory coming along?"

"It's about the same," Cole said. "I've been having headaches, though, and wondered if it was a side effect of the medication. Don't you think I'm healed enough to come off it?"

Parnell clasped his hands behind his head. "I'd give it a couple more weeks. You know it's dangerous not to finish a prescription."

"Did you hear about the trouble at Wells's house yesterday?"

Parnell lifted his brows in surprise. "No, what happened?"

Cole studied Parnell's reaction as he described the break-in, but Parnell's expression remained guarded.

"It's a good thing you happened along," Parnell said. "What's going on between you and Wells's widow anyway?"

"Nothing. She cleaned out her husband's office earlier and forgot some things. I simply stopped by to take them to her."

"I see."

"She's having a difficult time right now. What exactly happened to her husband?"

"I thought you heard about his boating accident?"

"I did. But she mentioned that he was an excellent swimmer. Did the police investigate the matter?"

"I believe so, but there was no reason to suspect foul play."

Except that part of Wells's work was highly confidential, and now files had been deleted and someone had broken into Megan's house and stolen Wells's files. "But I thought I was supposed to work with Wells on his research, yet the only project I've found that he was working on was one you said was scratched."

"The project was scratched because it failed." Parnell's voice sounded stern. "And I wouldn't go nosing into confidential or closed files. Not if you want to stay here for long."

Parnell stood and adjusted his lab coat, cutting off any more questions. "Are you ready to start seeing patients? When you start working with people again, your memory will probably return."

# Get FREE BOOKS and a FREE GIFT when you play the...

## LAS VEGAS
### GAME

*Just scratch off the gold box with a coin. Then check below to see the gifts you get!*

**YES!** I have scratched off the gold Box. Please send me my **2 FREE BOOKS** and **gift for which I qualify**. I understand that I am under no obligation to purchase any books as explained on the back of this card.

## The Harlequin Reader Service® — Here's how it works:

"I'm not sure I'm ready to take on the responsibility of counseling someone else right now."

"That's understandable. But why don't you tag along with me and sit in on a couple of sessions. It might help your memory regarding therapeutic techniques."

Cole nodded. He supposed it couldn't hurt. But Parnell's warning bothered him. And why did he have the feeling Parnell wanted him to tag along so he could keep an eye on him instead of help him?

AFTER MEGAN HAD TENDED to her morning's round of patients and taken a despondent Daryl Boyd to the solarium, she met April in the hall.

"Meg, where were you last night?" April fell into step beside her. "I called all evening."

She'd forgotten about April's nightly call. "I'm sorry. I...I got caught up in everything that happened."

"Sounds like a story there."

"It is." Megan pointed to the break room. "Let's grab a cup of coffee and I'll fill you in."

Five minutes later, April stared at her in shock. "Oh, my God, honey, what's happening? What do you think the intruder wanted?"

"I don't know. He didn't steal my jewelry but the policeman said I probably disturbed him. He did take some of Tom's files, though."

"Tom had files at home."

"Just notes of old projects. Nothing confidential." Unless he had a backup file about M-T.

"So, why didn't you call me? I would have spent the night so you didn't have to stay alone."

Megan stirred her coffee, avoiding April's gaze.

"Cole Hunter showed up. He was bringing by some things from Tom's desk and found me on the ground."

April gasped. "Don't tell me he stayed all night."

Megan shook her head. "No, I went to his place." When April simply gaped at her, she continued, "Nothing happened, April. The police were dusting my place for fingerprints, and he thought I might have a concussion and he is a doctor—"

"A very handsome doctor."

"A doctor who is suffering from amnesia."

"What?"

"You didn't know."

April sighed. "No."

Megan briefly filled her in on his accident while April retrieved her purse from the locker and brushed through her hair, removing a silver compact to check her lipstick.

A compact that was almost identical to the one Cole found in her husband's desk.

Megan paled.

"What is it, Meg? You're white as a sheet."

"Nothing." Megan sipped her coffee and backed out the door. "I just remembered I have to meet Dr. Jones for a consult. I'll talk to you later."

"Call me if you want me to come over and stay tonight."

Megan hurried to the door. "Don't worry. That won't be necessary. Cole arranged for a security system to be installed."

"Are you sure? I don't mind."

"No, but thanks. I'll be fine."

The hell she would, she thought. Not if Tom and

April had had an affair. Not until this whole mess was resolved and she knew Cole Hunter's true identity.

Not until she was safe again in her own home.

Furious at having to live in terror and uncertainty, she strode straight to Jones's office, determined to get some answers.

He was finishing with a patient, so she waited in his outer office, pacing back and forth.

"Megan." He motioned her in as his patient left. "What can I do for you?"

Ignoring his good looks and charm had always been difficult, but today she barely noticed them. "I…" Why had she come? She sank onto the love seat, weary.

"What is it? You look upset." He lay a hand on her shoulder. "Can I get you something? Coffee? Soda?"

She shook her head, knotting her hands in her lap. "I have to ask you something."

"Yes." He sat down beside her, so close his leg brushed hers. A little too close for her tastes. "You know I'll do anything I can to help you through this difficult time."

She instinctively backed away. "Then tell me the truth about Tom."

He squared his shoulders. "What do you mean?"

She inhaled a calming breath. "Is there any chance that Tom didn't die in that boating accident? That his body might have been mistaken for someone else's?"

A deep frown marred his handsome face. "Why would you ask something like that?"

Megan shrugged, deciding not to confide about Cole. "I've had some strange dreams."

"Dreams that he's still alive?"

"Yes."

"Megan, you know dental records don't lie."

"But the dreams seem so real."

"You work with psychiatric patients. You've learned about the stages of grief, the meanings of dreams, the tricks our mind can play on us when we want to deny the painful truth."

Megan's throat closed as she toyed with her wedding band. He was right, she did know those things. So how had she let Cole Hunter make her believe he could be Tom when she knew in her heart that Tom had died? When she had felt his loss the first day he had turned up missing...

COLE STUDIED THE WAY PARNELL worked with the patients, taking notes. The whole process seemed eerily familiar.

And not familiar at all.

His anxiety deepened with every patient. With every hour.

He wanted to check on Megan. He couldn't shake the feeling that she was in danger. And that at any second she might be taken from his life.

A loss he didn't think he could stand.

Even though he had no right to her. Especially if he wasn't Tom Wells.

APRIL MET MEGAN AS SOON AS she made it back to the nurses' station. Wanda and Brenda, two other nurses, left to dispense meds. "Meg, Connie called up and said a man from that security agency phoned. They're going to be at your house in half an hour and want you to meet them there."

"I thought they couldn't come until tomorrow."

April shrugged, barely lifting her head from the chart in her hand. "Guess they had a cancellation or something."

"But my shift won't be over for another hour—"

"Listen, I'll cover for you." April stuffed the pen behind her ear. "You have to get this security system installed."

Megan hesitated. Had she jumped to conclusions earlier about April? Dozens of women in Savannah probably owned silver compacts. And she and Tom had both given April a ride at some time; the compact could have fallen from her purse in his car. Or April could have dropped files off at his office and accidentally dropped the compact. After all, she and April had been best friends since nursing school. April would never hurt her.

"Go on," April said with a worried smile. "I won't rest tonight unless I know you're safe."

"Thanks." Megan gave her a hug. "I owe you one."

The phone jangled and April answered it, waving goodbye. Remembering her promise, Megan hurried downstairs to tell Cole she was leaving.

"Is Dr. Hunter in, Connie?"

Connie's fingers paused over the keyboard. "No, he's in a patient consult with Dr. Parnell. He's been trailing him all afternoon."

Megan fidgeted with her purse. Surely she'd be fine. She was just driving to her house to meet the security company. She wouldn't get out of the car until the man had arrived.

"When he comes back, tell him I left to meet that security consultant. He'll know what I'm talking about."

Connie nodded and resumed typing as Megan headed

to the elevator. The hospital halls seemed empty, Megan thought, especially the corridors of the office wing. Tension knotted her neck, and she massaged the sore spot as she exited the elevator. Seconds later, she stepped into the dim parking garage, grateful daylight still trickled into the basement, although the low cement ceiling and boulder supports blocked most of it. A quick check of her watch told her she had to hurry to meet the guy on time. She pulled her keys from her purse while she jogged past the first two lanes of cars.

But just as she reached the rental car and inserted the key, a gunshot rang out behind her.

# Chapter Eleven

Cole rushed down the stairs toward the garage anxious to catch Megan. Dammit, he told her not to leave without him. But Connie said she was on her way to meet the security consultant.

His nerves on edge, he bolted through the door to the parking garage when he heard a gunshot. The bullet pinged off one of the cement supports, must have ricocheted, and hit one of the car windows. Glass exploded, then shattered. He froze, scanning the dim interior, searching for the source.

Searching for Megan.

Another shot rang out, then a shrill cry.

Suddenly images of another shooting bombarded him. *Bullets flying. A gun being raised. A bullet piercing his back. Him reaching for a gun, firing…*

The images passed just as quickly as they came, leaving him momentarily disoriented. But another bullet pelted the top of a car, ricocheted off and bypassed his face by a fraction of an inch.

"Megan, stay down!" He spotted her white rental car and sprinted toward it, ducking low, weaving in and out between the other parked cars. Suddenly tires screeched and a dark sedan peeled out the exit. He took off at a dead run to catch it or at least get a license plate, but by the time he crossed the distance, the vehicle disappeared out of sight.

Heaving to get his breath, he jogged back toward the car. Megan was crouched on her knees by the driver's side, trembling.

He knelt beside her and helped her stand. ''Are you all right?''

She nodded, although the dazed look in her eyes told a different story. His own heart roaring with fear, he pulled her into his arms and held her, rubbing her back to calm her. She clung to him for several seconds, letting him absorb her shock.

''Who was it?'' she finally murmured against his chest.

''I don't know. All I saw was the tail end of a dark sedan but couldn't get a license plate.''

''What's going on here?'' The elderly security guard trotted toward them, tucking his shirt in his pants and reaching with a wobbly hand for his gun. ''I thought I heard gunshots.''

''Where were you?'' Cole snapped.

''I had to go to the john,'' the old man said, embarrassment heating his face. ''Is he gone?''

''Yes.'' Cole curved an arm around Megan. ''Let's go to the security booth. We need to call the police and file a report.''

''But what about the security company at my house?''

''I'll phone and ask them to wait.''

She squeezed his arm as he guided her to the booth.

''Sit down on that stool, ma'am, I'll get someone

right away.'' The old man phoned the local police station and Seaside Security's head while Cole paced the outer rims of the booth, searching to see if someone else lurked in the parking deck. He phoned the home security company on his cell phone. "Yes, I called earlier to arrange a system to be installed at Megan Wells's house." He gave the address. "You phoned to say you were sending someone out to meet Megan Wells this afternoon instead of tomorrow. Can you—what—you didn't call—" His worried gaze met Megan's. "No one is scheduled to install the system until tomorrow morning. I see."

He thanked the man, then hung up, his body tight. "Megan, who did you talk to?"

"I didn't,'' Megan said in a shaky voice. "April said Connie called up with the message."

Cole pointed to the security guard. "Can you call inside and ask April Conway and Connie Blalock to meet us here."

The old man nodded and did as he was instructed.

Five minutes later, April raced into the parking garage, Connie on her heels. "What's going on?'' April asked.

Terror streaked Connie's face. "What happened, Megan?''

"Someone shot at her,'' Cole said. "Megan said you gave her a message that someone from Steven's Security was meeting her at her place this afternoon."

"Yes, at four." Connie fidgeted with her hands.

"I called the company,'' Cole said. "They never phoned with a message.''

Connie gasped. April clutched Megan's hands, looking stricken.

"Who did you talk to, Connie?" Megan asked.

Connie stroked her neck in a nervous gesture. "I...I didn't get his name. The phones were going crazy, he sounded like he was in a hurry."

"You didn't ask—"

"No." Connie burst into tears. April tried to soothe her, glaring at Cole as if she'd picked up on the accusations in Cole's eyes. "He said to tell Ms. Wells they'd have a consultant meet her at her house at four." Connie's voice broke. "God, Meg. I was worried about you. You said someone had broken in, so I just thought you'd want to go home as soon as possible and get that security system installed, but if I did something wrong, something that put you in danger, I'm sorry..."

"I'm sorry, too," April said, tears lacing her voice.

Megan stood and hugged both women in turn. "Shh, I'm okay. You guys didn't know."

Cole frowned and waved toward the cop who was exiting his car. Megan might trust her friends, but he didn't.

Right now he didn't trust anyone.

MEGAN HATED THE FACT that this whole ordeal was making her distrust her own friends. Because for a minute, she'd wondered again about April. And even Connie.

"I'm so sorry," Connie said.

"You know I'd never do anything to hurt you," April said.

"I know. Listen, you guys, don't worry. I'm fine now."

The cop that walked toward them took in the scene with a scrutinizing eye. He stood slightly taller than

Cole, Megan noted, with jet black hair and blue eyes. Another officer, shorter and stout, with a receding hairline followed.

"Detective Adam Black, Savannah P.D. Someone called about a shooting?"

His voice was deep and rough, Megan noticed, thinking no one would mess with this cop.

Cole stared at the man, his face paling, almost as if he'd seen a ghost. "I had security call." Cole filled him in on the gunshots, then quickly described the car fire and break-in at Megan's house.

"The chief filled me in on the others," Detective Black said. "I've been out of town." He leveled a gaze at Megan. "I'm sorry about your husband, Ms. Wells. From now on, I'm going to be in charge of your case."

"All right." Relief spilled through Megan.

"I'll start checking for bullets," the other officer said.

"Tell me everything you can about each incident, Ms. Wells." Detective Black removed a pocket notebook. "No matter how small the detail, even if you don't think it's important."

"All right."

April stepped back into the shadows. "I'm still on duty. I should go back inside, that is, unless you need me."

"Tell him about the call first," Cole said.

Connie spoke up and relayed the phone call message.

April fiddled with the pocket of her nurse's jacket and reiterated her part.

"Thanks, ladies," Detective Black said. "I appreciate your help."

"Call me if you want me to come over later," April said to Megan.

"Sure."

Connie and April walked back into the building, huddled together. A twinge of regret pulled at Megan for even questioning her friends' behavior. She and April had always been close. April had been a bridesmaid at her wedding, and Connie wouldn't hurt a fly.

"When did these strange things start happening?" the detective asked.

"A few weeks ago. After my husband's death."

"Right after the trouble here, when the CEO died?"

"About six weeks afterward," Megan said. "How did you know about Sol Santenelli?"

"I was one of the arresting officers. Unfortunately Arnold Hughes escaped." Detective Black twisted his mouth into a frown. "Your husband was supposed to meet my partner, Clay Fox, the night he died. But they never met. At least not that we know of."

"Tom was meeting the police?"

"Yes."

"But my partner was killed that night." Detective Black removed dog tags from his pocket, spreading them across his palm. "We found these, but not his body. We think it was washed out to sea."

Megan's and Cole's gazes locked.

"Tom's body washed up on the shore a few weeks ago," Megan said.

"Which means Clay's could still be out there." Black shifted, a pained look on his face, and Megan realized he and this man Clay must have been close. "Do you have any idea why your husband might have agreed to meet my partner, Ms. Wells?"

Megan shook her head. "No. I was told Tom died in a boating accident. At first, I couldn't believe it. Tom was an excellent swimmer."

The detective's eyebrows rose. "Sounds familiar. About four years ago, a microbiologist named Jerome Sims died here, supposedly in a boating accident. Later we learned the company was selling Sims's research out from under him, so Hughes had him killed."

Megan's throat went dry. "Tom received a big bonus from CIRP and paid off some debts right before he died. I thought he might have been working on a questionable project."

"Do *you* know why Wells was meeting your partner?" Cole asked.

"Not exactly. Fox was investigating whether or not Arnold Hughes had survived." Black's mouth twisted into another scowl. "His body might have drifted out to sea also. But if he had someone else helping him, he could have escaped."

"You think Tom knew something about Arnold Hughes?" Megan asked.

Black shrugged. "Can't say for sure. But I'm certain that meeting got both of them killed."

COLE SENSED HE'D MET Adam Black before, but that was impossible.

Unless he had talked to him as Tom Wells.

Or Hughes.

He didn't want to consider that possibility, but he couldn't ignore it, either. If he wasn't Wells or Cole Hunter, and Hughes had survived and been given a new face and identity, he might be Hughes. But if he was, why wouldn't the doctors at CIRP who'd performed surgery on him have told him?

The detective's partner was missing also. Maybe....

"How do you know your partner is dead for sure?"

Guilt tightened Black's face as he stared at Cole. "If he was alive, he would have found some way to contact me. I checked all the hospitals for unidentified victims for the last few months and found none matching his description. Plus we found a substantial amount of his blood and skin samples on the rocks. His badge was on the shore, too."

"I thought you guys always went out in pairs."

"Normally we do." Black rubbed the back of his neck, his voice husky. "If he'd waited till I returned from my honeymoon, he'd still be alive."

Suddenly Davis Jones and Warner Parnell strode toward them, both with fierce expressions on their faces.

"What's this about a shooting?" Jones rushed over to Megan. "Are you okay, Megan?"

Megan nodded, but Cole stiffened at the solicitous way Jones raked his eyes over Megan.

Parnell directed his attention to Detective Black. "What happened? Did you catch the shooter?"

"No," Cole said.

"We're checking for bullets now," Detective Black added. He glanced at Megan. "Ma'am, I'd like to come by and talk to you tomorrow, after you've had a chance to relax."

"That's fine." Megan pulled away from Jones, but the doctor hovered close by her side.

Black headed toward the other officer who had already located one bullet and was bagging it.

"How did you find out about the shooting?" Cole asked Jones.

"April Conway came running in to my office, near hysteria. She also told me someone had broken into your house." Jones took Megan's arm. "From now on, you'll be escorted in and out of the building. And I'll see that security is put on your house."

"I've already ordered her a security system," Cole said.

"Nonsense. She's an employee of CIRP, and so was her husband. Seaside Security will install a system in her house."

"That's all right, Dr. Jones, I can use the other—"

"No argument. I'll personally see to it that it's done tonight. CIRP will foot the bill."

Cole had to admit he was grateful for Jones's prompt action in securing Megan's safety, but he resented the personal nature of his attention.

How did Megan feel about the man?

MEGAN WAS SO SHAKEN by the shooting that she didn't have the energy to argue with Dr. Jones. His take-charge attitude touched her, although she was surprised he felt so responsible for an employee.

"Come on, I'll drive you home, Megan," Jones offered.

"I'd like to take my car," she said, confused at Cole's silence.

"All right, then I'll follow you."

"Be careful," Dr. Parnell said. "And don't worry…we'll beef up security around the hospital as well."

Megan said goodbye to Dr. Parnell, then Cole, then

climbed in her car, aware Cole watched her every movement. Her hands shook as she drove home, but she reminded herself that she was safe for the moment. That soon a new security system would be installed on her house. That Detective Black seemed to be taking her situation seriously and would investigate the strange things that had been happening.

Shortly after she and Jones arrived at her house, Seaside Security pulled up. Jones gave them directions and the three men who'd come to install the system went right to work.

Jones cradled her elbows in his hands. "It'll take them a couple of hours."

"I appreciate your doing this, Dr. Jones. But you don't have to stay. I'm fine now."

"I intend to stay until the system is installed and you know how to work it." He gently lifted a hand and placed it on Megan's cheek. "I'm worried about you, Megan. I'll stay even longer if you want."

Megan's stomach quivered. She and April had joked that Jones would come on to anything in a skirt, but she'd never given him the time of day. She certainly didn't feel comfortable with his interest now.

She lowered his hand, and slipped backward. "There's no need. But I appreciate the offer."

"How about some dinner while the guys work?"

As if to defy her, Megan's stomach growled in protest. "My refrigerator's pretty empty—"

"I'll order some takeout Chinese. It won't take but a minute."

Megan swallowed, fighting nerves. "Fine, I guess."

She didn't intend to let her guard down though. Not that she was afraid of Davis Jones, at least not afraid that he would harm her. But fear of another kind fluttered through her. He had never shown much of an interest in her. Why was he so friendly now?

Was it true concern for her safety because she was an employee or could there be some other reason for his sudden attention?

COLE PARKED DOWN THE STREET from Megan's and waited. What did Jones have up his sleeve? He had seen the man leave Megan's place, then return less than ten minutes later with a paper bag and a bottle of wine. Damn, what was the man doing—trying to seduce her?

Fury rippled through him.

Sure, women probably thought the slick guy was good-looking, but he was a head-case. Then again, some women found a cocky attitude appealing.

Did Megan?

Was she succumbing to Jones and his charms?

Fisting his hands by his side, he fought the jealousy consuming him.

He had no right to be jealous. Megan was not his.

She had belonged to Tom Wells.

The only reason she'd spent time with him lately was that she thought he might be her husband. And she was in danger.

Had the questions he'd been asking put her in more danger?

The last remnants of sun faded and darkness descended over Savannah when the security team finally left. Traffic noises echoed from the street, and Cole reached toward his keys, ordering himself to go home. To leave her alone. To let Jones protect her. To stop adding to her problems.

But he couldn't make his hand turn the key. Ten long minutes later, the front door opened and Megan and Jones appeared. Cole ground his teeth as he waited.

Jones lifted a hand and brushed a strand of Megan's hair from her face, then gently kissed her cheek. Cole saw red.

Then Jones sauntered toward his car, looking smug, a self-satisfied grin on his face.

The long lonely hospital stay rose in Cole's mind to taunt him. No one had come to see him. No one had even called to look for him.

He had been utterly alone with the pain and the darkness.

Megan seemed to be the only sliver of light that had slipped into that black hole since then.

Instead of driving away, he opened the car door. Before he could convince himself it was a bad idea, he knocked on the door.

She opened it, her mouth parting in a small look of surprise. Or maybe a smile.

"I know I shouldn't be here, Megan," he said in a gravelly voice. "But I'm afraid I pushed Parnell today about Tom. My questions might have put you in danger—"

"I asked Jones about him today, too." Megan's soft voice floated over him, igniting the flame of desire that had been smoldering within him all night. "It's not your fault, Cole."

She moved aside and gestured for him to enter. As much as Cole told himself to turn and walk away, he couldn't resist. He closed the door behind him, then did what he'd wanted to do ever since he'd heard that gunshot in the parking garage.

He pulled her into his arms and kissed her.

"SOMETHING'S GOT TO BE DONE. They seem to have some kind of connection."

"Dammit, I know. Why the hell did your shooter try to kill her at the research center?"

"He didn't."

"What?"

"That wasn't my man. I don't know who the hell it was."

He paused to let that information soak in. "Then someone else wants Megan Wells dead."

"Apparently so."

"Well, hell, Maybe they'll do our job for us and we won't have to muddy our hands with this one."

A long tense silence followed. The other man's breathing rattled over the line. He wasn't happy. "I don't think the experiment's working."

"I'm afraid you may be right. But we need to keep Hunter alive long enough to find out where that disk is."

"Then get on it. That cop Black is back. He's bad news."

"I know. We have to find the disk. Then we'll get rid of them both." Megan Wells's pretty face flashed into his mind. He wrapped his hand around the pair of panties he'd taken from her drawer. Black. Lacy. Sexy. Closing his eyes, he imagined her wearing nothing but the silky underwear. Imagined his fingers touching her. Imagined making her his.

It was too damn bad she had to die.

# Chapter Twelve

Megan sank into Cole's arms, savoring the heat of his body and the strength of his embrace. His kiss was gentle, yet full of restrained hunger, sending a wave of passion skyrocketing through her. He cupped her face in both his hands and nipped at her mouth, then tilted her chin up with his thumb so she looked deep in his eyes. She saw the desire, the dazed sexuality of a man who wanted her, yet also the fear and uncertainty that he shouldn't be touching her.

The fact that he hesitated only magnified her desire.

She was starved for tenderness and love, aching all over from the surge of terror that had engulfed her during the shooting. Cole could erase that fear, that loneliness that threatened to drag her into the depths of despair. He could make her feel alive again.

"Megan, this is probably wrong." He traced one finger over her kiss-swollen lips. "But I can't help but want you."

"I know," she whispered hoarsely. "I...I want you, too."

A small smile tilted the corner of his mouth. Then raw passion fired his dark eyes, and he lowered his head and claimed her mouth again. This time, the gentleness fled as he deepened the kiss, his hunger growing as he pushed her lips apart with his tongue and thrust inside, licking and probing the warm recesses of her mouth. Megan moaned and clung to his arms, her own desire spiraling out of control when his muscles flexed beneath her touch. His hands tunneled through her hair as he dragged her closer, pulling her into the vee of his thighs where his muscled legs cradled her. His sex hardened and bulged against her own burning heat. Moisture pooled in her womb, begging for sweet release.

His hands kneaded her back, then drifted lower to cup her bottom and stroke her thighs. Megan groaned and dug her hands into his thick hair, her body thrumming with desire. As if he knew where she ached, he slowly moved his hand to her breasts and cupped her weight in his palm, then rubbed her nipple to a feverish peak between his fingers. She whimpered and kissed his neck as he lowered his head to kiss the tips of her breasts through her thin white shirt. He gently lifted the fabric, planting hot tongue-lashing kisses along her abdomen upward until he licked at the sensitive skin of her breasts. He had just reached for the clasp of her bra when the phone rang.

They both stilled for a moment, but Megan ignored it, flinging her head back as he undid her bra. Her breasts spilled into his hands and liquid fire blazed through her. With a moan of masculine appreciation, he played with the sensitive peaks, licking and suckling her. "You taste like heaven."

Megan clung to him, the joy of ecstasy just within reach, but the phone continued to trill until Cole pulled back and grabbed it. They both halted at the sound of the low voice. "You better stop asking questions about Tom's death or you'll be sorry. You'll find yourself in the graveyard, too."

Megan pulled away and stared at the phone in shock.

"Who is this?" Cole asked.

But the caller had already hung up, the dial tone wailed through the room like a siren warning of death. And the caller ID read unknown.

MEGAN WITHDREW INSTANTLY. Cole knew he had to let her go. He had already taken things too far between them.

He reached out to help her straighten her clothes, but she backed away. "I...I can't believe I did that."

Emotions flickered in her eyes, replacing the passion. Fear from the phone call. Wariness over their interlude. "Megan, I'm sorry. It was my fault. I got carried away."

Her gaze was amazingly steady. "No, I wanted it, too. But...but I shouldn't."

He recognized guilt in her voice, and gently traced a finger along her cheek. "You don't have to feel guilty. Tom may be gone, but you're here, alive, Megan. It's okay to go on."

"I know." But she still turned away. "It's just...it hasn't been very long. And..."

"And what?"

"I shouldn't want you so much."

Her admission stunned him.

"Why not?" He grabbed her arms and turned her to face him. "Because you don't know who I am. Because you don't trust me?"

''Because,'' she said in a low voice. ''Because it wasn't this way with him. At least not at the end.''

He swallowed, letting her words sink in. ''What do you mean?''

Megan paced across the room to the window and stared outside at the oak tree in the front yard. She wanted to avoid his question, avoid him the rest of the night, but she could no more run from what was happening here with Cole than she could the problems in her marriage with Tom. At least she owed him the truth.

''Tom and I met after he finished his doctorate. I had graduated from nursing school and was applying for a job here.''

''And?''

''And we worked together. We got along. We dated…after a while the next logical step was for us to get married.''

''Are you saying that you didn't love him?''

Her gaze flew to his, panicked and full of misery. ''No. I did love him, but…but now I'm not sure I loved him enough.''

''What do you mean?''

''We both wanted children. When I didn't get pregnant right away, our relationship changed. Everything became so tense.''

''And then?''

''Then the passion just died.'' She hesitated as if it cost her to admit the truth. ''I tried to make our marriage work, tried to feel close to him, but he poured himself into his work and his research. And there was never any time for us.''

''For romance, you mean.''

She nodded, tears filling her eyes. ''Don't you see?

I failed him, so I shouldn't want you now." She swiped at a tear. "If only I'd been able to give him a baby, he might not have worked so hard. He might not have been so obsessed with his projects that he didn't confide in me." Her voice took on a panicked note. "And he might not be dead."

A million questions bombarded him. What if he was Tom and he hadn't died? Would they be able to put their marriage back together?

But what if he wasn't her husband?

She had admitted that the passion had not been as hot between her and Tom…

"Megan, I don't know what's going to happen, what we're going to find out about Tom or the research center. And I don't know who is trying to hurt you. Not yet. But I do know that you aren't responsible for Tom's death."

She pressed her hand to her mouth, trying to gather her composure.

"But I will find out the truth about what happened to him, and who's trying to hurt you." He moved toward her but she backed away again. "And when this is all over, when we find out if I'm Tom or Cole Hunter or someone else, and that passion is still there, then we're going to see where it takes us."

Megan didn't reply, she was too shaken by his statement.

Instead she gestured toward the door.

"I can stay on the sofa if you'd feel safer."

She shook her head. "I'll set the alarm."

He studied her for a moment, then nodded and walked toward the front door. Megan followed him, praying he left without any more declarations. She needed time to absorb the volatile emotions and chemistry between them.

He paused, raised his hand and gently brushed her cheek with his palm. "Will you call me if you need me?"

Megan nodded, the tenderness in his touch eliciting another seed of desire to burst inside. But this time, she refrained from acting on her urges. She watched him walk outside, then closed the door and locked it behind him.

COLE WOKE WITH MEMORIES of Megan haunting him. And the fear that she was in danger because of him so strong he knew he had to do something.

He wasn't getting anywhere at CIRP, so he decided to go to Oakland and see what he might learn there. Maybe something would jog his memory. Maybe he really was Cole Hunter and the date on the article he was supposed to have written was a simple misprint.

He called her first to make sure she was okay. She promised to stay home all day with the security alarm set. Detective Black was supposed to come by later.

He took an early-morning flight and arrived at the Oakland facility by noon. After passing security, he spent an hour walking the grounds, but nothing seemed familiar. Not the stone structures that stood like fortresses against the backdrop of the dense forest surrounding it or the small river that backed the property.

His leg ached as he approached the main office. "I'd like to see Dr. Chadburn."

"Certainly, Dr. Hunter." The redhead secretary, an elderly woman in her forties, smiled. "He's been waiting on you since they buzzed you through security."

Cole hesitated before entering the other man's office. "Have we met, Ms.—" He checked the name plate on the desk. "Hargrave."

She fluttered her hand. "I'm afraid not. I just started here last week."

He nodded and entered the polished doors of the office, wishing for some tidbit of recognition. He found nothing. The office reminded him of his own at CIRP, although this was the office of an administrator not a research doctor. Furniture was much more expensive, the bookcases filled with business journals, and a wet bar occupied one corner.

"Dr. Hunter, what brings you back to Oakland?"

Cole decided to cut to the chase. "I'm still suffering from memory loss…I thought returning to my old workplace might stir up some memories."

The doctor smoothed down a fuzzy gray mustache. "I see. Nothing's returned?"

"Not much. I can't work full force until I get better, either."

"Have you thought about hypnosis?" Chadburn tapped a pen on the desk. "You might try that and see if it helps."

"I'll think about it," Cole said. "I would like to see my old office though while I'm here."

"Certainly."

A few minutes later, Cole surveyed the eight-by-ten-foot room, now occupied by a new doctor, but nothing struck a familiar chord.

"Of course, Dr. Porter ordered new furniture and had the office repainted, so it doesn't exactly look the same as it did when you were here."

Cole gritted his teeth in frustration. The rest of the

tour continued much the same. Occasionally a nurse or doctor turned narrowed eyes his way when Dr. Chadburn introduced him, but he didn't recognize a soul. With his new face, no one recognized him, either.

"I'd definitely talk to Jones about hypnosis," Chadburn said. "You're at the best place for treatment, Hunter. Take advantage of it."

Cole thanked him for the tour, then walked down the hall, his gaze scrutinizing the names on the doors. An elderly man wearing coveralls backed out of the room, pushing a broom.

"Sorry, sir." The man tipped his head back and leaned his small weight on the broom. "You new around here?"

"No, sir. I used to work here, but I've relocated." He extended his hand. "Dr. Cole Hunter."

The man staggered back, squinting over bifocals that needed cleaning. "What did you say?"

"I said I'm Cole Hunter."

"No." The man shook his head and clacked his teeth. "Dr. Hunter didn't have no children."

"What?" Fear sneaked into the old man's expression.

"I realize that. I'm sorry if it seems awkward, but I had an accident after I left here and had plastic surgery." He ran a hand over his face. "This face is new."

"Maybe so, mister, but you must have grown at least four inches. Cole Hunter that worked here was older, only five-eight at the most." He leaned forward, lowering his voice to a whisper. "And if you was Cole Hunter, you come from the grave."

"What are you talking about?"

"Man died five years ago. Went to his funeral myself and saw them put him in the ground."

Cole frowned, and headed to his car. He'd track down every graveyard in Tennessee if he had just to make sure the old man hadn't been confused. But in his gut, he feared he already knew the truth.

He definitely wasn't Cole Hunter.

So why had Jones and Parnell and Chadburn told him he was?

LATE THAT AFTERNOON, Megan sipped her third cup of coffee as Detective Black settled at the kitchen table. In spite of the new alarm system, she'd barely slept the night before. Nightmares of the shooting had haunted her.

Along with disturbing dreams of sleeping with Cole Hunter.

"Ms. Wells, what can you tell me about your husband's work?" the detective asked.

Megan indicated the sugar and creamer dish but he shook his head no. "He didn't discuss his research with me. Most of the work at CIRP is confidential."

"Did you have any idea what he might be working on?"

She explained about the files on autism and the notes on hypnosis. "I did see a notation about a project called M-T but I have no idea what the acronym stands for."

"You've searched his files here and at work?"

"The ones I can find. A few files seem to have missing sections, though; information had been whited out or deleted. And someone broke in and stole the things I had here." Megan's hands tightened around the cup.

"Do you know why my husband was meeting your partner?"

"No. Clay was following up on our investigation of Arnold Hughes. We've searched Clay's place but can't find anything specific." The detective sipped his coffee, a frown pulling at his forehead. "My guess is that your husband either knew something about one of the projects or research that was questionable. Or—"

"Or he knew something about Hughes?" Megan inhaled. "So you think Tom was murdered?"

"Probably."

"But why come after me?"

"Maybe whoever killed your husband thinks you have the same information he did."

Megan stood, frustrated. "But that's just it, I don't know anything. I'm a nurse at the center. I work with patients, not research. Although..." She hesitated, then told him about the three questionable patients' files. That two of them had died and one was still unaccounted for.

"I'll check them out," he said, scribbling down the names. "How well did you know Arnold Hughes?"

Megan shrugged. "Not well at all. I saw him at a few functions related to the center. I never had any personal connection with him."

"What about your husband?"

"He didn't socialize with him. And as far as I know, Dr. Hughes wasn't involved in any of Tom's projects. He and Sol Santenelli oversaw the center, but they didn't get directly involved in the projects." Megan hesitated. It felt like they were getting nowhere.

The detective stood and refilled his coffee. "Have

you heard anything to indicate that Hughes might be back?''

Megan shook her head.

"You have plastic surgeons at the center?"

"Yes." She thought of Cole and his recent accident. "Why would you ask about plastic surgeons?"

"If Hughes had survived the explosion and he'd been hurt, he might have needed it."

Megan swung a startled gaze to the detective.

"Is there someone here who recently had plastic surgery? Someone new to the center?"

Megan nodded, her heart hammering in her chest. "Cole Hunter. The man you met yesterday."

"Tell me about him."

"He just came to work for CIRP. In fact, Dr. Jones, the head of the department, said they'd hired him to work with Tom."

"So he knows the details of your husband's work?"

Megan traced a finger over the coffee cup rim. "No. He claims to have amnesia. He doesn't remember anything about his life as Cole Hunter." She hesitated, not sure how much to reveal. Then again she had to know the truth, and this detective might be able to help her find it.

"What if he doesn't remember because he's really not Cole Hunter?" He narrowed his eyes at her. "You don't think he is, do you, Ms. Wells?"

"I don't know. He's…he's not sure. He…he thought he might be Tom."

"Your husband? Why does he think that?"

"He had a car accident the same day that Tom turned up missing. He was supposedly on his way here and a truck ran into him."

"And he's recently had plastic surgery?"

"Yes. At the facility on Nighthawk Island."

"Do you think he's your husband, ma'am?"

Megan clenched the cup in her hands. "I...I don't know what to believe."

Detective Black exhaled. "Well, if he was your husband, I don't understand what reason the center would have in bringing him back here as another man."

"I wondered the same thing." She saw the suspicions in his eyes, and her heart pounded harder. "You don't think he could be Arnold Hughes, do you?"

## Chapter Thirteen

"It makes more sense than keeping Tom alive, giving him a new face and telling him he's someone else."

"But...but if Cole is Hughes, why would Hughes think he's Tom?" Megan hugged her arms around her waist. He couldn't be Arnold Hughes, not the man who had tried to kill that woman a few months back. Not the man who might have been responsible for Tom's death.

A sick feeling stole over her. She had allowed him to kiss her, had let him hold and touch her.

Wouldn't she have sensed it if he was inherently evil? If he was trying to trap her into giving out information? Or was she so needy that she'd fall into any man's arms who claimed to want her?

Adam rolled his shoulders. "I don't know."

"And why would the center tell him he's a man named Cole Hunter?"

"Maybe the amnesia is an act. Maybe he's just co-zying up to you to find out if you knew why Tom was meeting my partner."

The doorbell rang and Megan jumped, bumping into the counter as she sat her coffee cup down. "I guess

I'd better get that.'' The detective followed her to the door. "Who is it?"

"It's me, Cole. Can I come in, Megan?"

Megan's gaze flew to the detective's. What if Detective Black was right? What if Cole Hunter was Arnold Hughes?

COLE MASSAGED HIS UPPER THIGH to alleviate the dull ache as he waited on Megan to answer. He saw the unmarked police car and realized that Detective Black must be inside.

Good, at least Megan was safe.

His head was still reeling from visiting the cemetery and seeing the tombstone with the name Cole Hunter on it.

On the flight back, he had considered Chadburn's suggestion of hypnosis, but if the people at CIRP had lied to him, then how could he trust them not to mess up his mind even more if he relinquished control during hypnosis? They could brainwash him into thinking anything.

The door opened and Megan stared at him, her big blue eyes wide with fright. His heart vaulted to a stop.

"What's wrong? Did something else happen?"

Megan shook her head and moved aside to let him enter. Out of the corner of her eye, he noticed Detective Black scrutinizing him. Black leaned up against the brick fireplace while Cole took the love seat.

"What's going on, Megan?" Cole asked. "You said nothing happened, but you look shaken."

The detective answered for her. "Ms. Wells was just filling me in on everything. Her husband's death. Your arrival in Savannah at CIRP, and your amnesia." Detective Black gestured toward Cole with a crooked thumb. "Suppose you tell me what you're doing here, Mr. Hunter. That is, if that's your name."

Cole stared at him, long and hard, then at Megan. What else had the two of them discussed? Had they discovered something about him that he didn't know?

Exhaling a labored breath, he steepled his hands, planting his elbows on his knees as he leaned forward. "That's true. I have very few memories of anything the past few months. Even before."

"What memories do you have?"

"I…sometimes I faintly remember knowing Megan."

The detective seemed surprised by his answer. "Go on."

"There's not much else to tell. I woke up in a hospital room on Nighthawk Island a few weeks ago. The doctors told me I'd been injured in a car crash on my way here. I was supposedly relocating at CIRP to work with Megan's husband, Tom."

"Supposedly?"

Anger rippled through Cole. "Listen, Detective, if you think I'm pulling something over on you, you're wrong." He stood and paced in front of the window, well aware Megan tracked his movements. "I wish to hell I could figure this all out. I was told I had severe scarring so the doctors did plastic surgery on my face. My larynx was crushed along with my left leg. It took me weeks just to be able to speak again, and I still have a limp. Which is obvious."

"I wasn't questioning the fact that you were injured."

Cole stopped and met his suspicious gaze. "If you

think I'm lying about the amnesia, you're wrong. The doctors told me I transferred here from the Oakland Research Center in Tennessee. The only memories I have so far are of Megan.''

"You think you might be her husband, Tom?''

"Maybe.'' He was surprised Megan had confided that much.

"But if he is,'' Megan asked, "who did I bury?''

"The only way we can know that for sure is to ex-hume your husband's body, Ms. Wells.''

"They...they said it was mangled beyond recognition.''

The detective gave her a sympathetic look. "You'd be surprised at the sophisticated technology available to us. Don't worry, Ms. Wells. We'll find out who the man is.''

"You think he might be Hughes?'' Cole asked.

Detective Black shrugged. "Actually my sources suggest Hughes is still alive. I'm wondering though if the body Ms. Wells buried belonged to my partner Clayton Fox.''

Megan wrung her hands together. "But why would someone do all this?''

"If the center was involved in a cover-up, and they killed Tom and my partner, and Tom's body was washed out to sea, they might have made you think my partner's body was your husband's just to appease you. To keep you from looking further.''

"So if the body belongs to your partner, I might be Tom Wells,'' Cole said.

Detective Black raised his gaze to Cole. "It's possible.''

Cole was tempted to share the information he'd

learned at Oakland today about Cole Hunter with them, but he read the silent implications in the detective's eyes and held his tongue. Detective Black thought he might be the elusive Arnold Hughes.

And Black had put the same fear in Megan's eyes.

Would he know it if he was a killer?

"How exactly did Hughes die?" he asked, unable to help himself.

Black studied him as he spoke. "One of the doctors who worked at the center was my sister, Denise Harley. She was working on a classified project to help improve cognitive growth in children. Several foreign governments were interested in the research, but Santenelli and Hughes agreed to sell it to the Germans before the FDA approval came through. When my sister found out, they tried to kill her. Santenelli died during the arrest, but Hughes tried to flee on a boat. The boat exploded several thousand feet away from the dock."

Cole squinted, a headache suddenly piercing behind his eyes. Images bombarded him.

*Fire consumed the boat, licking the sky. Helicopters soared above. Men in uniforms dropped from above. Feet pounded on the wooden dock. Gunfire exploded, pelting the fiberglass hull. Bullets pinged and ricocheted. A scream tore through the air.*

Cole jerked his head up.

What the hell had just happened?

Had he just had a memory of the scene Black was describing?

But how was that possible if he was Tom Wells? Had Wells been at the scene?

If not, then what the hell had he just seen in his mind?

MEGAN WATCHED COLE'S reaction, disturbed by the implication that he might be Hughes. The telephone trilled, slicing into the already thick tension. Megan read the hospital number on the caller ID and hurried to answer it.

"Meg, this is April. Listen, Daryl Boyd is acting out again. He insists on seeing you."

"Did he say why?"

"No, but he's really out of control. I know you were taking the day off, but—"

"I'll come over in a bit. Just try to calm him down."

"I will. And thanks. I don't know why he's so taken with you, but he is."

Megan sighed. Sometimes patients connected with one nurse or doctor and refused to respond or cooperate with another. There was no rhyme nor reason, just something embedded in their own psyches. When she hung up the phone, both the detective and Cole were watching her.

"An emergency?" Cole asked.

"No, but a patient is asking for me. I told April I'd stop by later."

Detective Black stepped away from the fireplace. "Then I'll head out. I'd like to get that court order to have your husband's body exhumed as soon as possible, Ms. Wells."

Megan nodded. "I'll walk you to the door."

She felt Cole's eyes on her as she left the room.

The detective leaned against the door, lowering his voice. "You should be careful about that man, Ms. Wells. At least until we find out who he really is."

"I know." Megan gripped the doorknob. "But he

came to my rescue twice. The day the car caught on fire and the day of the shooting.''

Detective Black frowned. ''Did he really? It seems a little coincidental to me that he was the first one on the scene both times.''

''Are you implying—''

''I'm not implying anything. Yet. But I'd watch my back if I were you.'' He handed her a business card. ''Call me if you need me, or if you find out anything at all about Cole Hunter.''

WHEN MEGAN RETURNED, fear once again clouded her mind. ''I really need to go to the hospital.''

''Why don't I drive you?'' Cole said.

''That's not necessary. I—''

''Are you afraid of me, Megan?''

She froze, the edge of hurt in his voice surprising her. The detective's words echoed over in her mind. She *should* be afraid of Cole. But she sensed he wouldn't hurt her. At least not physically. Her heart was another story.

He couldn't be that awful man Arnold Hughes, could he? There had to be some other explanation.

''I swear I'm telling you the truth, Megan. I don't remember my past.'' He walked toward her, raised a hand and gently brushed her cheek with his knuckles. ''My mind is like one big black hole. You're the only light in that darkness right now.''

She searched his eyes and saw sincerity. He was also afraid, she realized, afraid of the truth.

''All right,'' she said softly. ''We'll ride together.''

Relief etched itself in the fine lines around his mouth. ''Thank you for trusting me.''

Megan set the alarm and followed him to the car. She didn't completely trust him, she thought.

But she had to find out the truth.

Even if it meant staying close to Cole. Even if it killed her.

COLE DROVE TOWARD THE CENTER, the day's events playing over and over in his mind.

"So, how did your trip to Tennessee go?" Megan asked.

"Not very well. Nothing seemed familiar."

"I can't imagine how frustrating that must be."

Cole clawed his hand through his hair. "It was strange. When I arrived, Dr. Chadburn treated me like I'd been on staff, like we were old friends. He even showed me the office he said I'd used when I worked there."

"Did you remember it?" Megan asked.

"No. The new doctor had it repainted and new furniture brought in, but the location, the outside of the center, it seemed so foreign. It was like I'd never been there before."

"Did you feel that way at CIRP?"

"No. That's what's so weird. I didn't recognize anything at Oakland, but I did sense I'd been at CIRP before. Catcall Island, Skidaway, they all seem familiar."

Megan twined her fingers together in her lap. "Did you talk to any staff members at Oakland?"

"I spoke to a few people in the hall but no one seemed to know me. Of course, I look different." Cole shook his head. "But I did run into this janitor who was shocked when I told him my name."

"Why? Did he know something about you?"

Cole hesitated, then angled his head and met her gaze. "Apparently he knew Dr. Hunter."

"And?"

"And not only is my face different, but apparently the real Hunter was a lot shorter than I am."

Megan stared at him, her eyes crinkling at the corner. "Did he tell you where to find the real Hunter?"

Cole nodded solemnly. "Oh, yeah. In fact I went to see him myself."

"What did he say?"

"He didn't say anything, Megan. The real Cole Hunter is dead."

Cole's hands tightened around the steering wheel as Megan's face paled.

"Which proves you really aren't Cole Hunter?" Megan asked in a choked voice.

"And that the people here lied to me." Cole imagined the different scenarios running through Megan's mind. He wasn't Cole so he might be Tom. Or maybe that detective's partner although Black seemed pretty convinced that guy was dead.

Or he might be Arnold Hughes.

If he was Hughes, then it was possible that he had killed Black's partner, Fox. And Megan's husband.

He shifted, the icy numbness of disbelief settling inside him. What if the guilt he'd felt at Wells's funeral had come from knowing he had murdered the man?

MEGAN'S NERVES REMAINED rattled for the remainder of the ride. She sensed Cole was equally disturbed and remembered earlier that she'd questioned his identity but that she was trying to trust him.

At least for now.

All the more reason for her not to get involved with

him on a personal level. Not to succumb to his darkly intense charm should he try to kiss her again.

"I want you to remember what I said earlier, Megan." His voice sounded grave. "I won't hurt you. No matter what we find out about my identity."

Even if they learned he killed Tom?

He pulled into the parking lot at the hospital and caught her arm just before she got out. "You do believe me, don't you?"

Megan searched his face again, and saw only concern and worry. Either that, or she was the worst judge of character on the face of the earth. So she told him yes, then they walked side by side into the hospital.

Megan had once felt content within the confines of the research center, safe with its security, and almost friendly with the people who worked there. Now, she found herself searching faces, wondering if someone she knew or trusted might have shot at her yesterday.

She hated the suspicions, the tension dogging her like some invisible demon.

As soon as they entered the psych ward, the quiet tension exploded into fear. Chaos erupted. Nurses bustled back and forth, whispering in hushed voices, an orderly ran down the hall, and an elderly volunteer sat in a corner vinyl chair crying.

Megan headed over to talk to her when April suddenly appeared around the corner. "Meg, oh, God, I'm glad you're here."

"What's wrong?"

April clasped Megan's hands in between her own. April's were ice-cold.

"Tell me what happened," Megan said.

"It's Mr. Boyd, Meg," April said in a stricken voice. "He committed suicide about a half hour ago."

# Chapter Fourteen

"What happened?" Megan asked, the numbness of shock settling over her. "Didn't you tell him I was coming?"

"Yes, I told him." April blew a strand of hair from her face. "He calmed down, so I left him for a few minutes in his room to rest. Later, one of the other nurses went in to give him his meds and found him." Her voice trembled. "It appears to be a drug overdose, but we won't know for certain until the autopsy."

"Dear God." Megan pressed a hand to her stomach. "I should have come sooner."

"It's not your fault," Cole said, "so don't blame yourself, Megan."

"He's right," April said, hugging Megan. "No one knew he was suicidal."

"But his behavior had been erratic—"

"He's schizophrenic, Meg. Of course his behavior was erratic."

"Still, I should have done more." Megan blinked back tears. "I knew he needed extra care."

"Megan, you can't think like that," April said. "We learned we're not God the first year in nursing school.

You did everything you could." She shook Megan slightly. "You even rushed to see him on your day off."

"This...all this craziness has to stop." Megan staggered backward, her control shattering. "It has to stop now."

"What are you talking about?" April asked. "What craziness?"

Megan had to escape the fear that had swept into her life since Tom had died and nearly stolen her senses. She needed to escape Cole Hunter.

"Take a deep breath," Cole said. "Inhale. Exhale. Come on and sit down, Megan."

She shook her head when he motioned toward the chair, but she did as he'd instructed and forced herself to do some deep breathing exercises to calm herself. Panicking wasn't going to help Daryl Boyd. Or bring him back.

Still, the accusations he'd ranted the last time she'd been in to see him echoed in her mind.

The fact that Tom's death had been called accidental, but now police suspected he'd been murdered. The microbiologist's death that had been similar five years ago. Cole's accident and appearance at Tom's funeral. The fact that someone had tampered with her car, then shot at her.

Was Daryl Boyd's death really a suicide or was it related to the other mysterious things that had been happening at CIRP?

COLE AND MEGAN SPENT THE next hour at a staff meeting Dr. George Ferguson, Jones's assistant, had called to discuss Daryl Boyd's alleged suicide. Apparently

Jones and Parnell were both away for the day at a medical convention in Atlanta.

"The police are checking the possibility that Boyd's death wasn't suicidal," Dr. Ferguson said.

"Did he leave a suicide note?" one of the nurses asked.

"Yes. The police are checking it out also, as a precaution, but it looks legitimate. His handwriting matches. There will be a full investigation, but meanwhile I hope our staff will keep all the other patients calm." His voice rose with authority. "Although I don't think Boyd had formed friendships with any of the patients at the center, be on alert for any patient who needs grief counseling. We don't want to mention the police investigation either and create a panic among the patients."

"Like they're not paranoid enough," one of the doctors muttered, earning a low rumble of chuckles from the staff, laughter which they all knew resulted from much needed tension release, not anything funny.

Ferguson cleared his throat. "Now, this episode brings us another problem. We need to double-check security regarding the dispensing of all medicines."

"How did Boyd obtain the drugs he supposedly used to kill himself?" Cole asked.

Ferguson eyed him over his clipboard. "We don't know yet, but we're looking into it. If he had assistance, rest assured we'll find out from whom and we'll deal with them."

The staff dispersed, huddling in various smaller groups to chat, others rushing back to duty or home depending on their schedules.

"Who was Boyd's primary psychiatrist?" Cole asked.

"Dr. Jones," Megan said in a low voice. "Although Tom treated him before that."

And Boyd had accused Cole of doing horrible things to him? Had he instinctively sensed that Cole was Tom? Had Tom performed some unethical type of treatments on Boyd? Was that the reason Tom had been so secretive?

"I think I'll hang back and talk to Dr. Ferguson," Cole said.

"I want to see how Connie is." Megan stuffed her hands in her pockets. "And then I'd like to take another look through Tom's files. We have to find his backup disk."

"I'll meet you at the office in a little while," Cole said. Hopefully Ferguson could give him some information on Tom Wells's work. He'd question him about the hypnosis treatments Wells had used, too. Maybe it was time he thought about taking steps to force his memory to return.

MEGAN WAS SURPRISED TO FIND Connie's door closed; she normally left it open during office hours. She knocked but no one answered, so she turned the knob. The door squeaked open and Megan slipped inside, frowning at the empty desk. Connie had probably taken a coffee break. She would wait and check on her, then she'd search Tom's files one more time.

Inside Connie's office, she paused to study little Donny's photo, his cherublike face resurrecting her own nurturing instincts, when a noise sounded from Tom's office. She froze and listened. Cole couldn't have ar-

rived that quickly; she'd left him waiting to speak to
Dr. Ferguson. The rattling continued. A footstep. A low
voice. Someone mumbling.

She tiptoed toward the door and peeked between the
cracks. Connie stood at Cole's desk, rifling through several files. The paper shredder churned and spit out the
remnants of whatever papers Connie had fed it.

What in the world was she doing?

Connie glanced up just as Megan rounded the corner
of the door. Her mouth flew open, her hands trembled.
"What…what are you doing here, Megan?"

"I was going to ask you the same question."

Connie bit her lip, that little nervous flutter of her
eyelashes a telltale sign. "I…I was getting rid of some
of Tom's old files. He asked me to clean them out before he died, and I never got around to it."

Megan raised a brow, waiting to see if she elaborated.

"I haven't been that busy since Dr. Hunter took over
so I've had plenty of extra time and I thought it would
make things easier for him." She halted as if she realized she'd lapsed into rambling mode, but Megan refused to let her off the hook. There were too many
strange things happening at the center to not pay attention to every detail. Instead she walked over and
glanced at the file folders, skimming the labels.

Daryl Boyd's name flew out at her.

"You were destroying Boyd's files?"

"No, of course not."

Megan picked up the folder and found it empty.

"That was a duplicate one," Connie said. "I con-
solidated his file into one." She indicated the drawer.
"It's right here if you want to see it. We never should

have had two files…that was a mistake. I was new and accidentally typed two different labels.''

Megan examined the file. Everything seemed to be intact. But what if she had shredded some papers about Boyd? ''I'm sure Dr. Ferguson and the people investigating Daryl's suicide will need to see this.''

''I figured they would,'' Connie said, her eyelashes fluttering anew.

Another glance at the folder and Megan read two more names. Fred Carson. Jesse Aiken.

Where had she heard those before?

The names she'd seen in Tom's notes—the patients who'd had adverse reactions to their medication and had later died. Another name, Harry Fontaine. The third man, still unaccounted for. What had happened to him?

The last file surprised her even more. Connie Blalock. ''You shredded your own file?''

A nervous laugh escaped Connie. ''Listen, Megan, I realize it's not the norm—''

''You shouldn't even have access to your own file.''

''But I haven't been a patient for a while, and Terry is making noises about suing for custody of Donny, and I was afraid he might get hold of them and use that information against me. With father's rights activists raising a stink lately, I was afraid some judge would ignore the fact that he was abusive, and I panicked.''

Megan didn't know whether to believe her or not, but Terry Blalock had been abusive. Tom and confided that much. She had seen the bruises on Connie more than once. Connie's ex-husband didn't deserve his son.

But even if she could justify Connie destroying her own file, what about the others?

She needed to see what had been in those files.

She struggled for a solution, then remembered the backup system the center used. A file room in the basement that contained duplicates of patient's files. It was worth a shot.

"Listen, Connie, you shouldn't destroy any more files, old or not, until Dr. Hunter gets a chance to review them."

Connie nodded, looking relieved not to be reprimanded or fired. She gathered herself and strode toward her own office. Megan silently memorized the numbers on the files in the trash and followed Connie back into her office.

After Connie locked Cole's door, Megan headed downstairs to the file room. She didn't want to believe that Connie might be connected to Tom's death or with Daryl Boyd's or the danger surrounding her, but she had acted suspiciously. And Megan wanted some answers.

COLE HAD TO WAIT IN LINE to speak to Dr. Ferguson. Meanwhile he studied the reaction of the staff. Most of the nurses seemed to have calmed although Megan's friend, April, seemed agitated as she answered Ferguson's questions about the day and Boyd's death.

Finally she turned to leave, her gaze nervous as it met Cole's. Then she disappeared down the hall.

"Dr. Ferguson, do you have a minute?" Cole extended his hand. "My name is Cole Hunter."

"Yes, Dr. Jones mentioned you were here. It's nice to have you."

"Can we step into the lounge for a minute?"

Ferguson gestured for him to lead the way and Cole

did. When they both had coffee, Ferguson turned to him. "What can I do for you?"

"Did Jones mention my amnesia?"

"Yes."

"Tell me about the hypnosis techniques Tom Wells was working on."

"I wish I could, but I haven't been here very long. I'm afraid Wells was already gone when I came to work here."

"Have you used hypnosis with amnesia patients?"

"Yes, if you're interested, I'd have to conduct a full exam first, though. I need medical charts as well."

"All right."

"Do you think you're ready for hypnosis?"

Cole shrugged. "I don't know, but I'm willing to give it a try. I need to figure out what happened in my past."

"All right, we'll schedule a time. I'll be out of town next week, so let's shoot for the week after."

Cole agreed. "Megan Wells claimed that her husband Tom treated Daryl Boyd the last few months before he died. When I first met Boyd, he mentioned some kind of treatment with a helmet? Do you know what he might have been talking about?"

Ferguson jerked his head sideways. Cole had noticed the nervous tick during his talk with the staff. "No. Boyd was paranoid—"

The fire alarm suddenly sounded, the wail piercing in intensity. The door flew open and a nurse poked her head in. "It's not a drill. This one's real. We have to evacuate."

MEGAN HAD JUST LOCATED the files on Carson and Aiken and had started searching for Harry Fontaine's when the fire alarm rang. Darn it. She wanted to find Connie's file, too, and see if she could learn anything about M-T. Hopefully this was just a drill.

Dust motes hung in the stale air, the scent of moisture strong as if the roof might have a leak somewhere that needed to be fixed, and a spiderweb dangled above her. She combed the rows, hurriedly searching the stacks for Cole's file. Footsteps pounded above her though and she halted. It sounded as if they were clearing the building.

An odd odor permeated her nostrils. Not moisture this time.

Smoke.

The fire was real. Somewhere close by.

Her heart jumped in her chest, skipping a beat. She ran toward the door, scanned the room and noticed a thin stream of foggy smoke curling through the bottom opening. Fear splintered through her. But she ordered herself to be calm. She was in a secure building. The fire alarm would alert the security. Firemen would arrive any second.

Reminding herself not to panic, she pressed a hand to the door, but quickly jerked it back. The door was already hot. A sob welled inside, but she swallowed it.

Frantic now, she glanced around the wall of files for another escape. No back door. No window. If a fire spread inside, the paper files would go up in a second. She had to get out. Take a chance. Run through the fire if she had to.

Even knowing the door was hot, she reached for the doorknob and tried to turn it.

But the door was locked. Megan choked on a sob.

There was no way out.

And not a single soul knew she had come down here.

COLE'S HEART HAMMERED as he helped the nurses and staff evacuate the thirty-something patients in the psych ward. Calming them and reassuring them that things were fine had been difficult, but since the fire had broken out in another part of the building, they had rationale on their side. Out of sight made it seem surreal, but the staff couldn't take any chances.

"Are we going to die?" an elderly woman shrieked as he pushed her wheelchair toward the exit.

"No, ma'am. Everything is fine. The firemen are already here."

"Mercy, is it the Fourth of July!" a man screeched.

"I got to save my cats," another woman shouted.

"Your cats are at home and they're fine," a nurse murmured patiently.

"Get those damn spies who bombed the place!" a deranged man yelled.

"They burning the witches?" another patient cried.

Nurses and volunteers combed the crowd trying to calm them while firemen raced toward the building, storming inside with rescue equipment to scope out the source. Emergency vehicle lights swirled in the cloud-covered sky, the lawn was a chaotic mess, filled with hospital beds, wheelchairs and staff, all staring as smoke fogged the lower windows and flames streaked through the first floor.

"We'll try to contain the blaze, folks, and hopefully have you all back inside shortly," a rescue worker announced over a bullhorn.

"You'll be fine here, ma'am." Cole settled the woman's chair beside another patient's. "I have to check on some other folks."

She nodded, squinting as if her hearing was impaired. He ran through the confusion, searching and shouting Megan's name, but couldn't find her.

"Have you seen Megan Wells?" he stopped to ask one of the psych nurses he'd seen talking to Megan earlier.

"No, not since the meeting with Dr. Ferguson."

His heart hammered as he continued to search. He found an orderly he'd seen on the psych ward. "Have you seen Nurse Wells?"

The man shook his head and Cole ran on. Finally he spotted April huddled by Jones. Oddly Jones had his arm around her in a comforting gesture, but Cole didn't have time to contemplate their relationship.

"April, have you seen Megan?"

April's eyes widened in alarm. "I thought she left."

"She went to check on Connie. Have you seen her?"

"There's Connie!" April pointed and Cole spun around to see Connie running from the building. He raced toward her. She looked wild-eyed and nearly collapsed as he reached her. He steadied her with his hands and caught the faint scent of smoke on her clothes.

"Connie, have you seen Megan?"

She shifted her gaze, tears blurring her eyes. "A little while ago. But I thought she left."

No, she wouldn't leave without telling him. Would she?

"Did she say where she was going?"

She shook her head. "No, I figured she went home. Maybe she's helping with the patients."

"I've already looked, she's not here. And she doesn't have a way home. I gave her a lift earlier." He scrubbed a hand over his face. "She said she wanted to look through Tom's files again."

Connie gaped at him. "She…she came in his office, but she left."

He struggled to think of where she might have gone. "Are duplicate copies of the files stored anywhere in the building?"

Connie's face paled. "The basement. There's a storage room down there." She slapped her hand to her mouth and pivoted, a low cry tearing from her throat. "Oh, my God. The file room is in that wing. If she went there, she might be trapped inside."

# Chapter Fifteen

Megan banged on the wall and yelled until her throat was raw, silently cursing herself for not bringing her purse with her. At least then she'd have her cell phone. Determined not to give up, she scanned the room for a backup system to open the door or another entrance, but found nothing. Damn. The smoke grew thicker, nearly filling the room. Once the fire crept inside, it would catch the paper and the room would be ablaze in minutes.

She took a calming breath but gagged on the smoke.

*Don't panic. Someone will come.*

*Only no one knows you're down here.*

The fire alarm was still ringing, though, she reminded herself. Firemen had to be here by now. Surely they would find her. Knowing smoke naturally floated upward, she dropped to her knees, coughing as more smoke wrenched the air from the dark basement room.

She scanned the room for something to create a noise and spotted an old metal ladder in the far corner. She crawled toward it, gasping and coughing. By the time she reached it, sweat trickled down her face and neck, and her limbs felt weak.

She yanked it down and dragged it toward the door. When she crossed the room, she grabbed the metal rungs and banged it on the concrete floor. Once, twice. A few more times. But exhaustion pulled at her, and heat pounded her from all sides, draining her. Smoke filled her lungs, suffocating and thick. She coughed, fighting the terror, but her eyes grew heavy. Her chest heaved as she struggled for air. She finally collapsed, unable to fight any longer. The bitter taste of death filled her mouth as her face met the cold hard floor.

COLE'S HEART POUNDED as he ran toward the building, but a fireman grabbed him and yanked him to a stop before he could move any further. "You can't go in there—"

Cole tried to jerk away. "I think a woman may be trapped in the basement file room."

"The basement is where the fire started."

"I know." Cole fought for calm. "You have to find her. She's a nurse here. Her name is Megan Wells."

He gestured toward the lawn. "Have you looked out there?"

"Yes, dammit, and she's not there." He pushed past him. "And if you won't look for her, I will."

The fireman chased after him, but Cole didn't stop. He ran down the hallway, tugging his shirt over his mouth to stifle the smoke. Seconds later, he dodged a small blaze in the hallway, found the stairs and sprinted down them two at a time.

"Wait!" The fireman followed, close behind.

"We have to get to her!" Cole shouted.

Flames ate at the basement in sporadic patches while several firemen hosed them down. Where was the file room? He scanned the hall, his pulse clamoring when he saw the fire spreading through the downstairs. A blaze crept along the wall, splintering wood and sending sparks flying. Heat poured off the fire, drenching him in sweat. Smoke rose like a heavy fog through the halls.

His chest tightened. Megan might be trapped behind the blaze.

"You think she's down there?" The fireman shoved an oxygen mask over Cole's face.

Cole nodded, his heart in his throat.

"Then stay behind me." The fireman suddenly jumped into motion, leading a path through the fiery blaze until they reached the file room door. He blasted the flames at the doorway with a fire extinguisher, and handed Cole an ax. Cole raised the ax and slammed it against the door, hacking at it over and over until finally the doorknob cracked and fell to the floor. His heart stopped as he shoved open the door.

Megan was lying on the floor unconscious.


MEGAN FELT AS IF SHE WAS floating. Floating on a lifeless sea of water. Drifting toward a bright light. A light that offered sanctity from the agony of her past. She lifted her hand and held it out, ready to take the path.

*Lead the way,* she tried to whisper. *I'm too tired to go on. Too scared. Too alone.*

"No, go back, Megan. It isn't your time."

The voice sounded familiar. Tom?

"*I love you, Megan. I'm sorry for putting you through this. But you have to move on now. You have to go back.*"

*No.*

*The light began to fade, the voice fell silent. Darkness*

*bathed the clouds. Obliterated the peaceful light. Swept her into its vortex. She was spinning. Spinning. Reaching out for something to hold onto. She tried to open her mouth to scream, but the whisper of another voice soothed her.*

"Shh, you're going to be all right now."

*Tom? No.*

"I'm so glad you came back to me, Megan."

*The voice sounded strangled. Deep. Husky. Worried. Cole.*

*She fought to open her eyes. Felt her eyelids flicker. A sliver of light broke through.*

*Her chest ached, though. Then she was coughing. Someone placed a mask over her mouth.*

"Breathe in. Breathe out. You'll be fine."

*A hand gripped hers. Strong. Steady. The whisper of a kiss tickled her hand. Took away the numbness.*

*She tried to smother the ache in her chest. Opened her eyes.*

Then she saw him.

Covered in smoke and smut. Sitting beside her.

"God, Megan, I thought I'd lost you."

Megan clung to his hand. She had almost died.

But Tom had been there. Saying goodbye. Telling her to move on.

She stared at Cole and tried to swallow, but a tear leaked out and rolled down her cheek.

Or had she just been dreaming about Tom because another man had come into her life?

COLE'S HEART CLENCHED. "You're fine, Megan. You're in the hospital. The doctors want you to stay overnight for observation."

Megan frowned and tried to speak, but another coughing attack assaulted her.

"Shh, don't talk. They're treating you for smoke inhalation. Your throat's probably going to hurt for a while. You need to lie back and rest. I talked to Detective Black and he'll drop by the house to question you about the fire when you go home."

A hint of a nod was her only reply. Then her eyelids lowered and she drifted to sleep. Cole pulled a chair up beside her and bowed his head, resting it on the bed, his hand still clinging to hers. He had no idea if he was a religious man but he murmured a silent prayer of thanks to the heavens. Then he closed his eyes and tried to block out the image of Megan lying unconscious on the floor.

And the realization that if they had been five minutes later, she would have died.

*THE BOAT ROCKED BACK and forth. Back and forth. Water pounded the sides, The purr of the motor cut through the night. Thunder rumbled from the ominous sky. He docked the boat, tied the anchor.*

*Searched the shadows of Serpent's Cove. A footstep sounded. Twigs snapped. A gunshot rang out.*

*It pierced his back and sent him spinning forward. Blood spurted from his mouth. He tasted bile. Saltwater. The tide rolled in. Sweeping him out. Waves crashed on the rocks. Soared over his head. Then darkness.*

*No, fire. An explosion. He had to escape the boat. Flames clawed at him. He lunged for the side. A gunshot fired. He raised his own weapon and fired back. The shadow of a man's body fell over the side.*

*He was going to die. He had to get the disk. Save*

*Megan. They would kill her to get to it. The car. He'd hidden it in the car.*

*No, he was on the shore. Someone was attacking him. Helicopters roared above. A fist connected with his face. Smashed his nose in. Pounded him again. Over and over. Blood spurted from his mouth. He tasted death.*

*He reached for the gun. Raised it and aimed. Saw the shadow again. He swayed. Dizzy. Spit out the blood. Lifted his arm. Fired.*

*And watched the man die.*

COLE JERKED AWAKE, his stomach rolling as the images from his dreams bombarded his consciousness. The dreams had made no sense. They were jumbled. Mixed up.

They had to be.

Because if they were real, if they were memories, then he had killed someone in his former life. Had he killed Tom Wells, Megan's husband? Or Clayton Fox, the detective Tom had gone to meet that night?

His phone rang. He jerked it up, his heart pounding.

"Hunter, it's Detective Black."

"Yes?" Had something happened to Megan?

"I found out something interesting about those three patients, Carson, Aiken and Fontaine."

"What?"

"They were all three prison inmates. Seems they traded their volunteer services for a special research project for an early release."

"And two of them died."

"Sounds like reason for a cover-up to me."

"What about Fontaine?" Cole asked. "Any word on him?"

"No, nothing yet."

"What was he in prison for?"

Black cleared his throat. "Murder."

Cole lost his breath. Fontaine had been a patient and was unaccounted for. And Cole had dreamed he was a murderer.

Could he possibly be Fontaine?

IT WAS LATE AFTERNOON the next day before the doctors released Megan. April had stopped by to visit on her way to work and so had Connie. But Cole insisted on driving her home. Megan was too exhausted to argue.

"Did anyone know you went down to the basement file room?" Cole asked as they stepped inside her house.

Megan hesitated in thought, then walked on into the den. "No. How did you know to look for me there?"

"I didn't. Not at first anyway." Cole rammed a hand through his hair. "I thought you'd gotten out when the fire drill started, so I helped the nurses evacuate the psych ward. When I got outside I couldn't find you." He paused, searching her face. Megan wondered if he could read the questions in her eyes. He continued anyway, as if he didn't blame her for asking. "I found April. She said she thought you'd left. I was frantic, then I saw Connie. I asked her about another storage area for the files, and she told me about the basement file room."

The scent of smoke still lingered on her skin. She

had to shower it off, wash away the haunting memories of being trapped.

As if he read her mind, he slowly approached her. "Are you all right?"

She knotted her hands, willing herself to be strong. "Yes."

"Did anyone follow you or see you go down there?" Cole asked in a low voice.

"No, not that I know of. Why?" She met his gaze. "You think someone started that fire to kill me?"

"Either that or to destroy the files you went searching for."

"Oh, my God." She struggled for composure. "Right before I went to the basement, I went to Tom's office. I mean your office."

"It's all right, Megan," Cole said with a small smile. "I know it's hard for you to see me there."

She nodded miserably. She was so confused. Yes, it was hard. But she was beginning to care for Cole anyway. Even if he turned out not to be Tom. But she shouldn't...

"So, what happened in the office?"

"Connie was sorting through the file drawers, shredding files."

"Shredding them?"

"Yes. I saw the names on the folders, Frank Carson, Jesse Aiken and Harry Fontaine. They were the same names I'd seen in some of Tom's notes."

Cole explained the detective's findings, his stomach churning.

"Tom and some of the other doctors actually used prisoners for their projects?"

"It looks that way. Since we know at least two of them died, they probably wanted to cover it up."

"Connie shredded her own file, too."

"Why would she do that?"

"She claimed her ex-husband, who is a real bastard," she added when he gave her a curious look, "was threatening to sue for custody of their little boy. She was afraid he'd use her background against her."

"Was there something damaging in her file?"

"Not that I know of. She was afraid being a patient would hurt her."

She thumbed another strand of hair from her face, wrinkling her nose at the brittle, smoky scent. "I guess I must have dropped the files when the fire broke out."

Cole pressed a hand to his temple.

"Now, what are you thinking?" Megan asked.

"It seems awfully coincidental that Connie acted suspicious, shredding files without talking to me, then you go to look for those files and you wind up getting trapped in a fire that started in the basement."

Megan read his silent message and shuddered.

He pulled her into his arms. "I'm sorry. I know Connie's your friend but—"

"But you think she may have tried to hurt me?"

"You said she wasn't stable before?"

"Yes, but she was living with an abusive husband. She was fragile and insecure." Her voice sounded weak. "Tom and I helped her escape that situation."

Cole exhaled wearily. "Maybe she doesn't have anything to do with it. It just seems suspicious."

"I hate this," Megan said. "I can't stand not trusting my own friends." Tears burned her eyes, but she blinked them away, pulling away from Cole as well. "I have to shower. I can't stand the smell of this smoke on me any longer.''

Cole's eyes darkened with concern. ''Megan, I am sorry.''

She simply nodded, then turned and headed to her room.

COLE SLUMPED DOWN on the sofa, exhausted and worried. He didn't like the fear in Megan's eyes or the lines of exhaustion on her face. He liked even less the fact that she was still in danger.

He lay his head back, the dreams he'd had while he'd waited by her bed in the hospital flashing through his mind. A week ago his head had been an empty hole. Now, it was filled with snippets of voices and explosions and gunfire, so many conflicting incidents he couldn't sort them all out. He had no idea which ones were real.

He mentally replayed the evening of the fire. He'd discussed hypnosis treatments with Ferguson, Megan had seen Connie shredding files, and gone to the file room... Was there more to this than the two patients' deaths? What exactly was the nature of the project those prisoners had volunteered to be participate in?

Who was he? Hughes? That other prisoner?

*Get the disk. They'll kill Megan for it. The car. He'd hidden it in the car.*

He jerked up, suddenly wondering if he'd just had a breakthrough. As soon as Megan showered, he'd ask her what she had done with Tom's car.

IN THE SHOWER, EMOTIONS finally overcame Megan, and she gave into them, allowing the tears to fall. Finally she dried her eyes and body, stepped out and pulled on a robe. She simply couldn't believe that Connie would hide something from her or hurt her. Cole hadn't seen Connie when she and Tom first met her. She was quiet, depressed and lacked self-confidence. She had never stood up for herself before. Tom worked miracles with her to convince her to leave her husband.

But Connie had been really upset over Tom's death. She'd guessed that Connie might have had a small crush on Tom, but had blown it off. Patients often fell for their therapist, it was a common pitfall and one most doctors recognized as such. But Tom had never treated her as anything but a patient.

Had he?

Megan frowned, remembering the lack of affection he had given her those last few months. She had wondered once or twice if his inattentiveness to her had resulted from an affair.

With Connie? Had the silver compact belonged to her?

A sick feeling slithered inside her at the thought.

No, Tom was an ethical man. He would never sleep with a patient.

But he had planned on meeting that detective's friend. What was his name? Clayton Fox. So Tom had known something about the center that he'd planned to take to the police.

Either that or he'd been involved in something illegal.

Had he decided to tell Fox about some secret project? Did it involve those two patients' deaths?

Exhausted from the questions, she decided to make some hot tea. Cole was waiting on her in the den, his expression troubled.

Her stomach did a funny dance when his dark eyes raked over her. She should have dressed. Her naked skin tingled at his perusal. Her nipples beaded to hard peaks, desire rippled through her, and an ache speared her from her head to her toes. She wanted him to hold her. To love her. To erase all this pain and worry.

He rolled his hands into fists, standing ramrod straight, but she saw the hunger in his eyes. He wanted her, too, but he was trying to resist. Trying to be the gentleman. Her protector.

Regardless of common sense, she was helpless to stop herself from moving closer. From inhaling his masculine scent and wishing he would fold those big, strong arms around her. From wanting him to forget about acting as her protector and be her lover.

"I remember something," he said without preamble.

"What?" That he was Tom? That they were married and they should be together?

"I think there's a backup disk that has something to do with Tom's work. He hid it in his car."

She clenched her hands around the belt of her robe. Had she just imagined the tension between them moments earlier? Had all the desire been on her part? Had she almost made a fool out of herself? "His car?"

"I had a dream, or maybe it was memories, anyway, there was something about a disk that has some important information on it. Where is Tom's car?"

Megan had considered selling it, but she'd let Tom's parents have it instead. "It's at my in-laws' house."

"How far away is that?"

"On the other side of Savannah."

"Will you call and ask them if we can come by and look inside?"

Megan hesitated. "What should I tell them? They don't like me very much—"

"Just tell them you left something in the glove compartment. Maybe some important insurance papers or something."

Megan nodded and picked up the phone. Her stomach knotted when Tom's mother answered.

COLE HEARD THE DISTRESS in Megan's voice as she spoke to her mother-in-law.

If he was Tom, the woman was his mother.

So why didn't he feel the burning desire to see or talk to the woman himself? To inform her he was still alive?

Because she obviously wasn't very nice to Megan?

Had Tom gotten along with his parents or had he detested them because they hadn't accepted Megan? A family break might explain the reason he had no memories of his parents. The reason he hadn't felt drawn to them at the funeral the way he had Megan.

She hung up the phone, agitation lining her already weary face. "She said we can come over in the morning."

Impatience flared, but the strain on Megan's face suggested the morning was soon enough. Tonight she needed to rest.

"Was Tom close to his parents?"

Megan shrugged. "They agreed most of the time. That is, on everything but me."

"Why didn't they like you?" Not that it mattered to him what those people thought. He moved closer to her, breathing in her freshly showered scent. The strawberry fragrance of the body wash she liked to use in her bath.

Her golden hair shimmered in the dim light and shadows of the room. His sex stirred.

"They were blue blood. I wasn't. For some people that's enough."

"Tom obviously didn't care." He sure the hell didn't.

Megan remained silent, emotions stirring in her eyes. He reached out and gently wiped a water droplet from her cheek. "But he had to have seen how beautiful you are."

Megan swallowed and met his gaze. He'd detected the hunger and need earlier, but he'd forced himself not to act upon it. What if Megan was only seeking comfort? If he followed up on the chemistry between them, would she hate him later?

"He had to have seen how strong you are."

"I...I don't know."

"He must have wanted you very much to have defied his family."

"I wondered if he was just in a rebellious mood."

"Oh, Megan." The sight of her lying unconscious in that smoky room tore through him. The memory of her almost dying. Of almost losing her. "Don't you see how utterly beautiful you are?"

His heart clenched. He wanted her with a fierceness that trapped the air in his lungs.

She released a shaky breath, her blue eyes searching his. The flicker of hunger lingered in their depths. No, he hadn't imagined it earlier.

Heaven beckoned in the sultry promises in her eyes. His finger traced her lip in an erotic whisper that heightened his own desire. Passionate surrender resonated in her quick intake of breath as he lowered his mouth to kiss her.

She tasted like sweetness, like sugar and spice and all the naughty things a woman should taste like. Fear had driven him to her, but passion drove him to keep her. To take her and make her his.

Not Tom's. This had nothing to do with Tom.

He plunged his tongue into her mouth and savored the warm way she opened to him as he dragged her into his arms. She cupped his cheeks in her hands and matched his rhythm, sinking against him with the utter surrender of a woman who wanted to be loved. A woman who needed him almost as much as he needed her.

If that was possible at all.

He paused long enough to clasp her face and force her to look into his eyes. "I want you, Megan, so much. But if you want me to stop—"

"No. I want you to make love to me, Cole."

"Because you think I'm Tom?" He regretted the question the minute it slipped from his mouth.

But he would never regret her answer, though it shocked him just the same.

"I want you even if you're not."

# Chapter Sixteen

Megan closed her eyes and sank into the moment. The feel of Cole's lips on hers. The warm sensuous taste of his tongue. The tender yet hungry way he wrapped her into his arms and held her.

It had been so incredibly long since she had been held by a man. And loved with the hunger that she felt in Cole's embrace.

Whether he was Tom or a stranger, she wanted his body, wanted to know him intimately the way she had known only one other man—her husband.

He was everything she had ever wanted. Needed. Desired.

And so much more.

His tongue swept over her lips, driving inside her mouth and torturing her with erotic thrusts. She groaned, teasing and suckling his lips while he thrust his hands into her hair and tangled it around his fingers. The low sound of hunger he emitted sent warm honey pooling in her abdomen, the burn of passion like an aphrodisiac flowing through her veins.

He suddenly swept her into his arms and carried her to the bedroom. Megan draped her arms around his neck and pulled him closer, her breath catching when he lowered her to the bed. He stroked her body with his, then gently lifted his weight and looked into her eyes.

The yearning, the whisper of his breath brushing her neck elicited a shiver of longing steeped with such intense pleasure it almost bordered on pain.

"I have to see you," he whispered. "I have to touch every inch of you."

Emotions welled in her throat as he tenderly undressed her, dragging gentle fingers everywhere her clothes had been, tracing a path of ecstasy with his hand and mouth, and awakening dormant senses that begged for release.

With a harsh masculine growl full of unleashed passion, he tore his own clothes off and flung them to the floor. Megan's heart pounded at the sight of his muscular body. Dark hair dusted his broad chest, tapering to a vee down his flat washboard stomach to his sex. She raked her eyes over him, over every hard plane and angle, over his long muscular thighs, the scars on his leg that hadn't yet healed, to the way his sex throbbed and jutted toward her, thick and hard and ready to take her to heaven.

Cole drank in the sight of Megan's beautiful soft body. Delicate might describe her, but undeniably sexy was the word that rose to taunt him. He wanted her hard and fast and anyway he could have her.

But he couldn't take her that way or he might scare her.

He let her look, his sex throbbing bolder at her heated gaze.

"I have a few scars," he murmured in a husky voice.

She pressed a finger to his lips. "You have a magnificent body."

A lazy grin curled his lips. He kissed her finger, then drew it in his mouth and suckled the tip. She flicked her tongue out and he couldn't hold himself back anymore. He traced a path across her face, her nose, her lips with his hands, then his mouth, then cupped her breasts in his hands and rubbed his leg over hers. She answered by twining her legs with his and stroking his calf with her bare toes. He thought he might lose it then.

With a guttural groan that tore from deep inside his soul, he lowered his head and licked at the rosy tips of her breasts, suckling and feeding on her until she cried out his name.

"Please, Cole."

"Please what?"

"Please…please make me yours."

A smile ballooned in Cole's chest as he rolled her nipples between his fingers and dipped one hand lower to tease the soft contours of her stomach, her inner thighs, then licked his way to her feminine sweetness.

"Cole—"

"Shh, I want to taste you." His mouth found her and he fed his starving soul with her honeyed gift until she finally sighed his name and cried out in oblivion.

Then he claimed her as his, the way he desperately wanted, taking only the briefest of seconds to pull on protection. He pushed inside her, wrapped her legs around him and thrust to her core, whispering her name and riding her until he felt her shatter around him. Only then did he allow himself to bare his own heart by pouring himself into her.

MEGAN PULLED THE SHEETS to her neck, her insides shaking from the intensity of their lovemaking.

She knew, *knew without a shadow of a doubt,* that Cole Hunter was not her husband.

The first time had been full of passion and longing, as if they had both waited a lifetime for such fulfillment. The second time tender and sweet. The third time raw and primal.

Tom had never touched her like that or groaned her name as if he'd die if he didn't have her.

Cole turned lazily beside her and propped his head on his hand, then reached for her hand, a cocky satisfied grin on his face. Megan clutched the sheet tighter.

"You're not Tom Wells."

Cole's hand dropped to the bed, his smile fading. "Why...do you say that?"

"I...I just know." Tears clogged her throat.

Cole sat up, his mouth tightening. "How can you be sure now—"

"I was married to Tom, Cole. I slept with him, I knew his body. I knew how he touched me." She licked her dry lips. "You aren't Tom."

He stared at her, a dozen emotions flickering in his eyes. The silence stretched long between them, filled with threads of tension that snapped and crackled in the air. She heard his labored breathing, saw him struggling for an answer.

"You don't think you could have forgotten—"

"No." Megan grabbed her robe from the end of the bed, slipped it on and stood, knotting it furiously. "A woman doesn't forget that kind of passion."

"The kind you had with Tom?" His voice sounded low. Angry. Hurt.

"No." She dropped her head forward in defeat. "The kind I just shared with you."

He was off the bed in a split second, standing in front of her, naked and strong and handsome. He coaxed her to look at him. "Megan, you're saying that it was more passionate with me?"

She closed her eyes on a sob. "Yes."

He had no idea how to respond except for an odd giddiness that ballooned inside him. "Well…"

"Don't sound so smug." A tear dribbled down her cheek. "Just because Tom wasn't as passionate or loving or tender or…or—"

"Or what, Meg?" He tipped her chin up with his thumb, slowly stroking the soft skin beneath. "He didn't make you hungry for more?"

She shook her head. "I did love him, though."

He dropped his hand, snapped his jaw tight. "I know." A hint of anger edged his voice. "No matter how much I want you, I'll always have to fight that ghost, won't I?"

She pressed her hand to her mouth. "It's not that."

He grabbed her then and kissed her again, unable to stop the desperate urge to hold her. "It's not what?" he whispered when he finally pulled away. His expression softened as if he saw the truth in her eyes. "It's guilt, isn't it, Megan? You don't think you should want another man so soon after Tom died?"

"No." She ran over to the dresser and picked up a card. "He gave this to me a week before he died. We had our problems but this letter meant he wanted to try to work things out. But we never had the chance."

"That doesn't mean you can't have a life with someone else."

"Is that what we're talking about, Cole? A life?" She heard the hysteria rising in her tone. "How can we have a life or a relationship when you don't know who you are. Just look at this handwriting. It's Tom's, is it yours?"

He examined it, then grabbed a pen from the dresser and scribbled her name, copying the message word for word.

*Megan, I want to start over. Meet me tonight. Love, Tom.*

They both stared at the words, then each other, the truth staring back. Cole definitely wasn't Tom. Then who was he?

COLE INSTINCTIVELY SQUEEZED Megan's hand, bracing himself for her withdrawal. And the shot of sexual attraction that rippled between them. Just her simple touch ignited his senses and made his body hard. It had only been hours since she'd lain in his arms, naked and sated.

He wanted her again.

But he had no right. Not until he discovered the truth about his identity.

Because if he was Arnold Hughes, and he had killed Megan's husband, she would hate him. And if he was that prisoner, Fontaine...

He couldn't be a cold-blooded murderer, could he?

"I know this is hard for you, Megan. But I hope you know I would never hurt you." At least not on purpose, he added silently.

But instead of rejecting him, Megan clung to his hand. He wasn't sure if her lack of withdrawal resulted from his comment or the fact that they pulled into the

Wells's driveway. Seconds later, the overbearing couple reluctantly agreed to let Megan look inside the car.

"I appreciate this, Mr. and Mrs. Wells," Megan said. "I'm trying to get the insurance tied up and all our papers transferred to my name."

"Yes, well, that's a good idea," Mr. Wells said.

They obviously didn't intend to foot the bill for any of Megan's expenses, Cole thought, a bitter taste in his mouth. And judging from their half-a-million-dollar estate, they could easily afford it. The stingy snobs.

"Who is this man with you?" Mrs. Wells peered down at Cole, her patrician nose wrinkled.

"Cole Hunter." He shook their hands. "I came to Georgia to work with Tom."

"Actually Tom was supposed to leave him some disks for work," Megan added. "I've searched the office and couldn't find them, so I was hoping Tom might have left them in the car."

Mr. Wells crossed his thin suited arms. "Well, be quick. We'll be inside. Bring the key in when you're finished."

Megan agreed and Cole waited until the couple left the five-car garage before he opened the door. He searched the glove compartment and under the seats, but instincts told him the disk was better hidden.

*Check the back seat. Tom cut a seam in the fabric beneath the back cushion and taped it shut.*

He hurried to the back seat, knelt down and ran his fingers over the underside of the cushion. There. He had it.

He turned to Megan and smiled. "I think this is what we've been looking for. Maybe we'll finally get the answers we need now."

Still, as he and Megan drove back to her house, questions plagued him. How he had known where Tom had hidden the disk if he wasn't Tom?

"I WANT TO GO WITH YOU to read the disk," Megan argued, when Cole dropped her at her house.

"No, you're not going back to the center today. Not after what happened yesterday."

"But—"

"No buts." He gestured for her to sit down.

Too tired to argue, she complied.

"First of all, someone shot at you in the parking lot, then you almost died in a fire yesterday. You're staying home with your security alarm set."

"Cole—"

"Don't argue, Megan." His tone brooked no argument. "Besides, Detective Black is supposed to come by and question you about the fire."

"When did you talk to him?"

"When you were asleep at the hospital. He said he'd stop by this afternoon."

"All right. But I want to know what's on that disk."

"I'll be back," he promised. He gave her a last soulful look, then disappeared out the door.

Megan watched him leave, a knot of anxiety gathering inside her. What was wrong with her?

Cole might be that awful Hughes man, or a former prisoner, a murderer. Yet, she still ached to go after him.

"HI, CONNIE."

"Dr. Hunter." Connie jerked her head up as if he'd surprised her. "How are you?"

"Good." He automatically covered the inside of his

pocket with his hand, feeling for the disk. Remembering that Connie had been shredding files from his office before the fire, he closed the door and inserted the disk into the computer.

He sat for a moment and stared at the screen, his hands fisted, his breath tight. He sensed there was more to the project than two prisoners' deaths. He only hoped this disk revealed the reason why Tom Wells had been meeting that detective.

Would it tell him who he was?

He hesitated, half afraid to continue.

What would he do if he learned he was Arnold Hughes, that he had killed Megan's husband and that cop? Of if he was that prisoner? Would he able to face Megan again after making love to her?

"DETECTIVE BLACK, COME IN."

"Ms. Wells. I came to the center yesterday about the fire. Are you all right today?"

"Yes. A little tired still, but I'll be fine." She sighed. "I just want this whole mess over with."

Detective Black leaned against the fireplace. "Wanna tell me what happened?"

Megan explained about finding Connie shredding files, then about her trip to the basement to look for those files.

"You didn't tell anyone where you were going?"

"No."

"Did you see anyone along the way?"

"A couple of nurses in the hall, but no one who paid any attention."

He made a smacking sound with his mouth. "Found

out that patient Boyd had an overdose on Pancurinoium bromide.''

''That seems suspicious.'' Megan explained about his rantings. ''Pancurinoium bromide is used in surgery. Daryl Boyd wasn't scheduled for any kind of surgical procedure.''

''Do you think he might have been involved in that research project?''

''M-T?'' Megan twisted her hands together. ''I don't know. There is one reference in his chart that he might have been on Nighthawk Island.''

''Maybe he's the missing prisoner, Fontaine.''

Megan tried to digest that possibility. That might explain his death, that is if it wasn't suicidal.

''Do you know anything specific about that project?''

''No.'' And Megan still couldn't believe Tom had gone along with something so unethical.

''Where's Hunter?''

''We found a disk in Tom's car. He went to the center to study it. He thinks Tom might have hidden it because he planned to give it to your partner the night he died.''

''I'd like to know what's on it. Wait a minute.'' He snapped his fingers. ''How did he know where to find it?''

''He said he remembered.''

''So he still thinks he may be your husband? Or he's psychic now?''

Megan sighed. ''He's not my husband.''

Detective Black waited expectantly, eyebrows arched expectantly.

Megan darted into the bedroom and brought back the card. She refused to tell him she had known because she'd slept with the man. "His handwriting...it doesn't match Tom's."

"I see." He studied the handwriting. "You do want to find out who he is, don't you?"

Of course she did. Didn't she? But what if he was that man Hughes? What if he had killed Tom? And Black's partner?

"Do you have an idea who he is?"

"A hunch. But we need some proof. Can you get the pen Hunter wrote with, ma'am?"

Megan felt as if she was betraying Cole, yet they both needed to know the truth. If he had killed Black's partner, the detective had a right to know. "Yes. It's in the bedroom."

"Do you have a plastic bag you could put it in? I'll check it for prints."

Megan's breath caught, but she nodded. A few seconds later, she returned and handed it to the detective. Soon they would know the mystery of Cole's identity, she thought as she watched the detective leave.

Then what would they do?

COLE SCANNED THE CONTENTS of the disk, his mind spinning. He didn't understand some of the technical jargon, another sign he wasn't Tom Wells. Part of him hated the fact that he wasn't Megan's husband, yet a small part of him was grateful.

He didn't want Megan to want him because he was her dead husband returned to life.

He wanted her to want him for himself.

Of course, if he discovered he was Arnold Hughes, the man who might be responsible for her husband's death, or if he was Fontaine, a convicted murderer, she would hate him.

He knew instinctively he had taken a man's life before and prayed he wasn't Fontaine. He had had a dark side. He had just been ignoring it in hopes that he was Megan's husband.

He skimmed the information on the disk, his eyes narrowing as he read the term Project Brainpower.

What the hell was that?

He read on.

*Genetic research to improve intelligence is under way. Plans for the project focus on enhancing cognitive learning through genetic engineering. Research conducted by Denise Harley.*

Hmm, Detective Black's sister. Black had mentioned she had worked at the center.

*Her research was incomplete but a special team is in place to complete the project.*

Then he zeroed in on Tom Wells's work on hypnosis.

*Certain drugs, Cognate and its derivates, are being tested to stimulate memory cells for Alzheimer's patients and have proven effective in maintaining short-term memory problems for other dementia disorders. More specifically, I'm working with patients who have repressed memories due to traumatic experiences suffered in their youth. So, far, results are inconclusive, but fifty percent of test subjects to date have expressed significant improvement efforts in recovering those memories. It is my theory that the patient will not overcome his mental disorder until he has remembered and dealt with the experiences that created the break in his emotional state in the beginning.*

He skimmed further, his heart pounding when he discovered another project, the one Megan had mentioned M-T.

*Closely related to my work, the center has approved a classified project called M-T, which strives to isolate specific types of memory cells, those affecting cognitive memories and intelligence from emotional ones, so they can be transferred to another person. Think of the implications for the intellectually challenged or severely mentally deficient person. Also, memory cells from those with superior intelligence might be preserved and transferred to others so that the intelligence will not be lost. Future plans include isolating memory cells related to artistic talents, musical abilities, etc. in an effort to preserve the geniuses of the world.*

M-T. Memory Transfer. Cole froze, his hands tightening on the desk as he contemplated the implications and how far the scientists might go to carry out their experiment. As the ramifications set in, fear settled in his gut.

Dear God in heaven, could they have possibly conducted one of those experiments on him to alter his memory? But how would they make him forget his real past?

He skimmed further and saw another notation—head of project: *Arnold Hughes. Three inmates from the state penitentiary agreed to become human subjects of the drug in exchange for early release. Unfortunately two suffered fatal side effects. Hughes has ordered a cover-up, but seeking other subjects for surgical study. Fontaine still under study.*

Cole tensed. Where was Fontaine? In the psych ward somewhere? On Nighthawk Island. Or was *he* Fontaine?

Or Hughes?

If Hughes had survived that explosion and wanted to return, what better way than to have plastic surgery and return with a new identity? Had Hughes offered himself as a human subject in his own research study and allowed the doctors to transfer Wells's memories to himself?

"THE SITUATION IS COMPLETELY out of control. Hunter went to Oakland. Chadburn covered for us, but it seems he met this stupid janitor. Wound up at the graveyard and saw Hunter's grave."

"Dammit to hell. But setting fire to the center was never in the plan.

"That wasn't my doing, just like the shooting. You know I'm not that sloppy."

"Whoever is helping us is getting in the way. I say it's time to bring in Ms. Wells and Hunter."

"You don't want me to get rid of her for good?"

"No. Not with that cop Black snooping around again. He caused enough trouble before." A heavy sigh, then he continued, "I have a better idea."

"Yeah?" So did he, but he doubted his partner would go for it. He wanted Ms. Wells for himself before they did anything to destroy her beauty. Just the thought of her lying next to him, beneath him, his hands wrapped up in that pretty blond hair sent fire through his body. If there was a way to keep her alive and get Hunter out of the way...

"Just bring her in and I'll fill you in on the plan."

"I'm outside her place right now. Black just left and Hunter's not here." He reached for the door handle and opened the door, letting his black boots hit the pavement with purpose. "I'll have her to you soon."

And maybe if his partner agreed, he would have her for himself after they finished with her.

MEGAN'S HEAD ACHED from thinking about the trouble surrounding her. She swallowed a couple of painkillers, chased them with a glass of water, then slowly walked back to her bedroom, trying to piece together the events of the last few weeks and make some sense out of them.

But nothing made sense.

She had come to Savannah to work, had met Tom and fallen in love. Or thought she had. Maybe she'd been searching for that security she'd so desperately craved all her life, and he had represented security at the time.

An ironic chuckle escaped her.

Nothing about her life right now felt secure. And it all seemed to stem from Tom and his research. When this nightmare ended, she should move away. Find a job where there were no memories of Tom.

Or Cole Hunter, whoever he turned out to be.

She lay down on the bed and flipped off the light, grateful for the darkness and the quiet. But just as she drifted off to sleep, the telephone jangled. Groggy but thinking it might be Cole, she reached for the phone on the nightstand, but a hand clamped around her arm just before she picked it up. The shadow of a man's face hovered over. She tried to push him off of her, but he pressed a cloth over her mouth, and a bitter smell filled her nostrils. Chloroform.

She kicked and fought, but the chemical sucked her in and she fell into nothingness.

# Chapter Seventeen

Cole let the phone ring a dozen times, his nerves on edge when Megan didn't answer.

She'd promised to stay at home with the security alarm set. He checked his watch. Even if Detective Black was still there with her, she would answer the phone.

Maybe Black had gone and she was in the shower. No, she had just showered before he left. Maybe she was asleep.

He hated to wake her if she was, but she needed to be on alert. Plus he wanted to tell her he planned to confront Parnell and Jones, so if he turned up dead, she should go to the police and reveal Cole's suspicions.

On the off chance, he'd dialed the wrong house, he punched in her number again and let it ring and ring. Damn. Ten times later, he called Detective Black's number. Maybe he'd send a car to check on Megan.

"Savannah Police Department, how may I direct your call?"

"I need to speak to Detective Black."

"He's not in, may I take a message?"

"Yes, it's urgent. Can you radio him and tell him to

check on Megan Wells. Better yet, you may want to send a unit there—''

''Who is this?''

He scrubbed a hand over his face. ''Cole Hunter. Detective Black knows who I am. Just give him the message. Then tell him to call me on my cell phone.'' He recited the number and hung up.

Figuring the disk might be his only bit of evidence, he searched the room for a place to hide it, finally slipped it between a crack in the underside of the wooden desk, then strode down the hall toward Dr. Parnell's office. It was time the doctors gave him some answers.

And this time he wouldn't settle for anything but the truth.

A DARK HEAVINESS ENGULFED Megan, trapping her in a den of fear. She tried to open her eyes, but her lids refused to move. Where was she? What had happened?

A dull throbbing pain beat a steady rhythm inside her skull. She had to sit up. But the second she tried to move, something pulled against her, holding her down. The sharp jab of a needle, pricked her arm. She peered through hazy eyes. White walls. Steel drawers for medical instruments. An overhead light for surgery. It seemed so familiar.

The strong scent of antiseptics filled her nostrils. She was in the hospital somewhere, but where?

And why? Had she been in an accident?

She fought through the haze, memories surfacing. Her husband's death. Cole's appearance. The attempts on her life. Daryl Boyd's death. The fire. The disk Cole had found that had belonged to Tom. The phone ringing. Then someone grabbing her...she'd passed out. And woken up to a rocking motion. A boat.

Where had they taken her?

She jerked, a cry tearing from her throat that never moved past her lips. The bindings trapped her to the cold steel table. Tears welled in her eyes and ran down her cheeks but she was helpless to wipe them away.

"Keep her sedated," a deep male voice said.

"You think this will work?"

"We'll make it work. And once she regains consciousness, she won't remember anything."

"Nothing?"

"Not even her own name. She'll be as incoherent as some of our worst patients."

"How will we explain her condition?"

A chuckle rumbled from the first man. "We'll say she had a nervous breakdown after her husband's death."

"Won't that cop Black be suspicious?"

"He'll never be able to prove anything. And once we take care of Hunter, there won't be anyone left to interfere or ask questions."

"Then the project can be considered a success after all?"

"Right." He traced a finger over her cheek, wiping away her tears as if he was a friend, not her enemy.

Megan shuddered.

"Too damn bad she had to be so nosy. But I'm glad we don't have to kill her." He traced a finger over her mouth. "Don't worry, Megan. This won't hurt. In fact, you won't feel a thing." He ran his finger along her jaw, then her neck. Nausea flooded her. "And you won't remember anything that's happened."

Anger warred with terror as she struggled to open her eyes and put a face with the men speaking. She'd rather die than be turned into a vegetable. But whatever drug they'd given her was working. A tingling, then numbness seeped through her veins, stealing the life and fight from her. Fear closed around her, boxing her like a caged animal.

The death of her future flashed through her mind. Now she would never know who the real Cole Hunter was. She'd never be able to tell him that she'd fallen in love with him.

The chance for a happy marriage was over. And the chance for the family she'd always wanted... It would all be wiped away just like her memories.

COLE KNOCKED ON PARNELL'S office door, shifting onto his stronger leg as he waited. The seconds ticked by, but no one responded. Frustrated, he knocked again, but received the same response. He took off to Jones's office, irritated at the empty office.

His gut tightened with a bad premonition.

He had to find them and force them to explain the Brainpower and M-T experiments. Find out if he was one of their subjects.

If he was Hughes or that prisoner.

He gripped the door handle, then poked his head into Jones's secretary's office. "Do you know where Dr. Jones is?"

The young brunette paused, fingers on her keyboard. "I believe he went to the lab."

"The lab? Can you be more specific?"

She shrugged. "Out on Nighthawk Island. Can I leave him a message?"

"No." He remembered the place they'd kept him after his surgery. He would find the answers there.

He phoned Megan again and was surprised when Detective Black answered. "Where's Megan?"

"She's not here," Black replied, his voice hard.

"Where the hell is she?"

"I don't know." Black hesitated. "But signs indicate she didn't leave here of her own free will. Someone turned off the security code."

Cole cursed. "I'm on my way to the lab on Nighthawk Island." He relayed the information he'd learned about the research projects Brainpower and M-T.

"You think you were one of their subjects?"

"Yeah." His chest constricted.

"Apparently those guys, Carson and Aiken, were subjects, too. They died because of an adverse response to the medication."

"What if they planned to do the same thing to Megan? Or what if they…" He couldn't finish his sentence. Couldn't make himself even think about losing Megan for good.

And if they found out he was Hughes or Fontaine….

It didn't matter. If they did, he'd deal with the consequences. The fact that Megan would hate him. But he couldn't deal with her death. He'd turn himself in first.

"I'll get backup," the detective said. "Wait, there's something I have to tell—"

"No," Cole said. "I'll meet you there. They've already tried to kill her twice. We can't waste a second." He hung up without waiting for a reply.

A few minutes later, he passed through security and commandeered a driver to take him to Nighthawk Island.

"I'll have to call for clearance," the security guard said.

Cole nodded. If he didn't get it, he would go anyway. Somehow.

But seconds later, the guard hung up and grinned. "Got it, sir. I'll have you there in a few minutes."

Cole nodded. Maybe he was wrong about this whole thing. On some kind of wild-goose chase. If Jones and Parnell were hiding something, why would they agree for him to come?

Unless it was a trap.

He clenched the boat hull, his mind spinning.

A trap?

Hadn't he felt like he was walking into a trap the night of his accident?

Bits and pieces of memories flooded him.

*He was pulling up at Serpent's Cove. Anchoring the boat. Walking the shore. Searching shadows. A twig snapped. Footsteps. Had he fallen into a trap?*

*Were they after him? Or after the disk?*

*Megan. Megan was in danger. They would kill her to get the information he had been ready to give that cop.*

*He raised his gun to fire. A bullet pierced him in the back.*

*No, someone was beating him.*

*He saw the explosion. The boat erupted into flames. Heat scalded him. Flames licked at his feet. He dived over the side.*

*The sea grabbed him and dragged him out. Sucked him into the tide.*

Cole jerked up. Again the memories had been Tom Wells. But he wasn't Wells. He knew it in his gut. The other memories, memories of shooting someone—were they Fontaine's memories?

Or Hughes's? Was he at the boat the night Hughes supposedly died?

"Sir, we're here." The guard collected Cole's cell phone. "You can't use that on the island. It's against the security policy."

The driver docked the boat and Cole gestured to the security guard that greeted him. "I need to see Dr. Jones and Parnell. They're expecting me."

The guard led him across the island to the main facility, a cement building that resembled a fortress. Newly renovated, most of the space was empty, but he recognized it from his own stay at the hospital.

"This way, Dr. Hunter." Another guard led him through the corridors and security to a surgical wing and lab area that brought memories of his own long hospital stay back in vivid clarity. The sterile cold walls. The stainless steel table and instruments. The foggy faces of nurses and doctors during those first few weeks when he'd been too incoherent with the pain and drugs to know who was even treating him. The terror when he'd realized his face was bandaged. That he might be scarred for life.

The fear of not knowing his own name. Or how he had gotten there.

The desolate loneliness of having no family or friends to visit.

He never wanted to be that lonely again.

But if he didn't find Megan and rescue her...

"Hunter, we've been waiting on you."

Cole grimaced at the Parnell's angry scowl. "Follow

me. I think you'll find this experiment rather interesting.''

Like the spider following the fly, Cole thought, only this fly wasn't an innocent victim.

They escorted Cole into a room with glass windows that overlooked a surgical room, equipped with all the latest modern equipment, including a stainless steel table that looked cold and frightening.

Then they wheeled Megan in on a gurney and his heart locked in his chest as rage trapped him in its meaty claws.

''WHAT ARE YOU PLANNING TO do to her?'' Cole asked in a harsh whisper.

''Erase her memory,'' Parnell said without batting an eye.

''Is that what you did to me?''

Parnell grinned. ''So, you've figured that much out.''

''Who am I then? Hughes? That cop who was supposed to meet Tom Wells? Or that prisoner who traded jail time to be one of your subjects?''

''Who you are doesn't matter. What matters is that our experiment on you failed.''

''What do you mean?''

Parnell studied him. ''I suppose I might as well fill you in. It's not like you'll remember any of it later.''

Cole nodded, stalling for time. Maybe Detective Black would arrive before they did anything to Megan. He glanced through the window and stared at her. She was lying so still beneath that white sheet. Tears streaked her pale face, and they'd strapped her arms down. Fury roared through him. She'd obviously been drugged. What else had they done to her?

"Project M-T was designed to isolate cognitive memory cells and transfer them to another person. Wells headed the project. Think about the ramifications for the mentally impaired person. The minute one of our geniuses of the world died, we could transfer that intelligence to someone else."

Cole shook his head. They were crazy.

"But why kill Wells if he was your lead scientist?"

"He had an attack of conscious. Went to meet this cop to spill his guts." He sucked air through his teeth. "Actually we never meant to kill him. But since he died…well, we decided to use you as a part of our research study and give his memories to you."

"You did all this through a surgical technique?"

"That combined with hypnosis and medication."

"The pills you prescribed?"

"They enhanced the posthypnotic suggestions we gave you after your surgery."

And when he'd stopped taking them, other memories had intruded. Memories of another life, of being another man. Of killing someone…

"It's brilliant really. The Mozarts of the world, the Einsteins, we'll be able to preserve those minds so they could continue contributing to society."

"Unbelievable," Cole said. "You actually believe society would benefit from this?"

Parnell nodded. "I have no doubt. Unfortunately we haven't quite mastered the isolation of the cells so when we performed the technique on you—"

"I didn't remember the technical aspects of Tom Wells's work."

Parnell snorted in disgust. "Such a disappointment."

He darted a gaze at Megan through the glass. "But you did seem to have a strange connection to Wells's wife."

Cole felt as if he'd been punched in the gut. When he'd read the research, he had entertained the idea of such a project, but to think these scientists had actually performed the experiment on humans, on *him,* sickened him.

And now they wanted to do the same thing to Megan.

He had to stop them.

Even if he died trying.

"I can't let you do that to Megan. She doesn't deserve this."

"You can't stop us now."

Cole spun around to argue, but Parnell pulled out a gun and aimed it at his chest.

# Chapter Eighteen

Megan fought against the haze of drugs and the restraints. She had to escape. She had to tell Cole what was going on.

Had they wiped out his memories the way they planned to do hers?

A movement flickered in her peripheral vision. A surgical mask. A man. His face was fuzzy.

"Just relax, Megan. It will all be over soon."

She recognized the voice. Jones.

Panicking, she pulled against the restraints, crying out when they snapped her arms back painfully. The door squeaked open behind her.

"What the hell are you doing bringing him in here?"

"I thought he might like to watch."

Megan strained to see, but the men were too far away.

"Megan, hang on, honey."

Cole?

"This is crazy, gentlemen. You've already carried things too far." Cole's husky voice penetrated the haze around her, soothing her. "I've already contacted Black. He knows where we are. He suspects you have Megan."

Parnell cursed.

Jones laughed. "It won't make any difference. All he'll find is a confused Megan." He chuckled. "In fact, when she wakes up, she'll be infatuated with me. You'd be amazed at what a few hypnotic suggestions can do."

Megan struggled again. He was sick. She had never liked him. She wouldn't, no matter what he did to her. A person could resist hypnotic suggestions, couldn't they?

"I don't think so," Cole said, his voice furious. "She will never be with you, Jones. Not after the things you've done."

"Don't you dare judge me," Jones growled. "I'm a genius. No one else could have accomplished the things we have with M-T."

"Because no one else is that sick and twisted." Megan heard footsteps and realized Cole was moving closer to Jones. "No one else is so unethical they would commit murder to preserve their own overinflated ego."

Megan startled as a scuffle broke out. Jones yelled an obscenity, a loud grunt of pain followed, and she heard fists pounding against bone. She struggled to move her arms again, fighting for her own escape. But her blood ran cold when a gunshot pierced the air. Another loud grunt and a thump followed. She froze, listening. One of the men had hit the floor. But who?

Had they killed Cole?

COLE MANAGED TO KNOCK Jones to the floor. He ducked and dodged the bullet from Parnell's gun, turned and karate kicked the weapon from Parnell's hand, then swung back and kicked him in the stomach. Cole snatched the gun from the floor, rolled to a stop by the surgical table and stood. Memories rushed back but he didn't have time to deal with them. Other fights. Gunfire. The air force. He had been a soldier. His name...

Loud voices punctuated the silence. The guards were on their way. They had to escape before they found them.

He hurriedly unfastened the restraints around Megan's wrists. "Megan, are you okay, honey?"

She moaned and opened her eyes. "Cole, you...you're alive?"

"Yes, baby, and we're getting you out of here." He slid his arm around her waist, furious when he realized she was wearing a hospital gown beneath that sheet. Who the hell had taken off her clothes? What had they done to her before they brought her here?

"Are you hurt, Megan?"

She shook her head. "Just dizzy from the drugs."

He wrapped the sheet around her, scooped her into his arms and ran toward the door. Footsteps sounded from the hallway, and he jogged the opposite direction. Megan clung to his shoulders, burying herself against his chest. A bullet pinged off the hall wall behind him and ricocheted above them. Another hit the glass window of the office door he'd just passed. Glass shattered. Megan jerked in his arms. He passed two corridors, and another office door, saw the staircase exit and took it. Running as fast as he could, he barreled down the steps. The footsteps pounded louder, closing in on them.

Winded from the run, he heaved a breath and pushed open the concrete door, searching for a place to hide. Two helicopters roared above them and he froze, the wind from the propeller whipping dust around them. A voice boomed out from the bullhorn. "This is the police."

Cole froze and thanked the heavens. Megan's fingers curled against his chest. "You saved my life, Cole."

A slow smile curved his mouth. "My name isn't Cole, Megan. It's Clayton Fox." He hugged her to him. "But you can call me Clay."

A tear rolled down her cheek. "You're the man Tom was meeting the night he died."

Cole's stomach lurched. He had finally remembered his identity. But even though he wasn't the horrible Arnold Hughes or that prisoner, if he hadn't dogged Tom Wells for information, Megan's husband would still be alive.

MEGAN WATCHED IN MUTE shock as the police handcuffed and arrested Dr. Jones and Dr. Parnell. She still couldn't believe that two physicians had gone to the lengths they had to preserve their research project.

And that Cole Hunter was actually a police detective.

Not a doctor or scientist at all.

Tom had planned to meet him the night he had died. So Tom had been one of the good guys. At least in the end.

Cole—no, Clay—patted her hand as if they were two strangers, his gaze guarded. "Are you all right, Megan?"

"Yes." She met his gaze, her heart thumping. What was he thinking? "You were there when Tom died?"

"Yes."

"Will you tell me what happened?"

He nodded, solemnly. "But first I have to talk to

Black. Then I'll take you home. That is, unless you'd rather one of the other policemen drive you?''

Was he so ready to be finished with her that he hoped she'd say yes? Did he blame her and Tom for what had happened to him? ''I'll wait.''

A small smile flickered, then disappeared. ''I'll be back in a minute.''

She watched him walk away, his stride purposeful, his big board shoulders and arms so thick and strong she longed for them to embrace her. Would he ever hold her again?

Or would he walk away once he took her home?

If he did, she would never feel the same kind of passion in another man's arms as she had felt in his.


CLAY SLOWLY APPROACHED Adam Black, his heart in his throat. Tidbits of his past life flashed back in painful clarity. The night Adam had gone after Hughes and Santenelli. The night Adam had married his new wife, Sarah.

The night he had met Tom Wells to get the disk. The gunshot that had most likely killed Tom Wells.

Black looked at the chopper where the police had just secured Jones and Parnell. ''Listen, Hunter, there's something I have to tell you. The fingerprints…'' Black paused and grinned sheepishly. ''I took the pen you wrote with at Ms. Wells's house, anyway, the fingerprints—''

''Belong to Clay Fox, your partner.''

Adam broke into a grin. ''You remembered?''

Clay nodded, his hand rubbing his face. ''Yeah, partner. I may not look the same, but I'm back.''

Adam threw his arms around him and pounded him

on the back. Clay chuckled, then sobered and said in a voice thick with emotions, "I've never been so glad to see you in my life, Black."

"So, THE BODY THE POLICE exhumed was definitely Tom's?" Megan asked, two hours later when she and Cole—Clay—had settled into her house. She still felt slightly groggy and weak, but the lingering effects of the drugs Jones had given her were slowly wearing off.

Still, she shivered at the thought of how close she had come to having her memory erased.

"Yes." Clay brought her a hot cup of tea.

Megan's hands trembled as she accepted it, the slight contact with his warm hands like a balm to her wounded soul. He noticed the shaky movement, though, and visibly tensed, pulling away to sit in the chair across from her.

"You wanted to know about Tom, about the night he died?"

"Yes." She sipped the tea. grateful for the soothing moisture. Her mouth was so dry it felt like cotton. Probably from the drugs.

He clasped his hands, leaned forward and braced his elbows on his knees. His dark eyes looked troubled. Haunted. "My memories are still scattered," he said in a gruff voice. "But I spoke with him a couple of times at the center. I was trying to get a lead on Hughes, to find out if anyone had heard if he'd resurfaced."

"And had they?"

"I never found out. But Tom seemed disturbed. When I pushed him, he backed off." He ran a hand over the rough stubble of his beard growth. "Then he contacted me a couple of weeks later. Admitted something was going on that shouldn't. Said it had gone too far.''

"The experiments with M-T?''

"Yes. He was going to give me the disk that night.''

Megan stared into the tea. "So they killed Tom because he intended to turn them in?''

Clay nodded. "They didn't mean to kill him. The shot that got him was meant for me. They only planned to alter his memory.''

"What?''

Clay's expression was grave. "They needed to get rid of me, not Tom. They wanted his knowledge about the research. When he died instead of me, they decided it was the perfect opportunity to try out their new project. They'd get rid of Clay Fox, and save Tom's memories. They figured if they gave me a whole new identity and I didn't figure it out, then the project was a success.''

"God, that's crazy. I didn't know it was even possible.''

"Apparently it didn't work as they expected.'' He released a disgusted grunt. "They tried to isolate cognitive memory cells, but the experiment failed. Some of the emotions Tom felt for you carried over, too.''

Had all his feelings for her belonged to Tom? And now that his own memories had returned, had his desire for her faded as well?

CLAY WATCHED MEGAN, struggling to decipher her reaction, but he couldn't read the myriad of emotions glittering in her expressive eyes. He was confused himself, more memories filtering through the darkness. But a few holes in his past loomed big and wide, like a canyon of emptiness. Parts of his childhood. His hometown.

He needed to recover all of his past. Or as much of it as he could before he could move on with his life.

For weeks, he'd been living his life as one man. Courting a dead man's wife.

What did his future hold?

He wanted Megan to be in it. But could she forgive him for setting up the meeting that had cost her husband his life? Even if she hadn't thought he was Tom, she had spent time with Cole Hunter, the psychiatrist, not Clayton Fox, the cop?

"I…it looks like the danger is over, Megan."

"I suppose so."

"I guess I should go, then. Let you get some rest."

"All right." She walked him to the door, pulling a blanket around her shoulders.

He hesitated in the doorway, breathing in her soft feminine scent one more time, memorizing her features, the way her lower lip protruded slightly when she frowned, the way those vibrant blue eyes changed with inflection as her emotions pingponged back and forth.

"What are you going to do now, Clay?"

He shrugged. "Try to get my life back together."

"Have all your memories returned?"

He shook his head. "Bits and pieces. I guess it'll take some time."

"What about hypnosis?"

He had talked to the Dr. Ferguson at the hospital, but he wasn't sure he'd use anyone at CIRP. "Maybe I will."

He gripped the doorknob, a bead of perspiration trickling down his neck. Soft light from the hall lamp bathed her face, outlining the curve of her nose and shimmering off her blond hair. Images flooded him—images of her lying in bed with that hair spilling around her shoulder. Of her cradled in his arms, of her smiles of ecstasy when he'd made love to her.

"Thank you for everything, Cole...I mean Clay."

The sound of the other man's name on her lips reminded him of the bizarre circumstances that had brought them together.

He didn't want her thanks. He wanted her love.

But that had obviously belonged to her husband.

A knot tightened in his throat, and he couldn't help himself. He reached out, cradled the back of her neck with his hand, pulled her to him and kissed her one more time. A real Clayton Fox kiss he hoped she would remember.

Although this time, he was afraid the kiss meant goodbye.

MEGAN SET THE SECURITY system, an aching loneliness echoing through her. For the past few days she and Clay had been together around the clock. Now, he had disappeared from her life, and the house felt empty.

Just as it had when Tom had first left.

Only different.

She and Tom had been married, while she and Clay had been what? Lovers? Drawn together through stolen memories?

The dreams she'd had about Tom had been so real— had he returned through Cole to tell her that he loved her? To tell her to move on?

Her angel collection had been shattered by the person who'd broken into her house. But Clay had surfaced, like a real-life angel, to protect her. Or had his detective instincts driven him to search for the truth and be her guardian?

Bittersweet reminders of Clay filled the house now. His scent lingered in the air just as the feel of his hands lingered on her skin.

Her gold wedding band shimmered in the lamplight. She had slept with Clay; it was time to accept that her marriage to Tom had ended. Slowly she slipped the band off and placed it in her jewelry case beside the silver chain Tom had given her. As she closed the case, she knew she was closing the chapter on her life with Tom.

Thoughts of the night she'd spent with Clay filled her mind again. The pleasure and passion she'd experienced with him had been so intense. Would she ever see him again?

A cold chill engulfed her, and she burrowed deeper into the afghan. As she climbed in bed, she imagined the afghan was Clay's big strong arms. And her pillow she imagined as his shoulder.

## Chapter Nineteen

The next two weeks passed in a miserable blur for Megan. She dragged the last of her summer clothes out and packed them away, her mind still sorting through her emotions.

She had settled her insurance claim and bought a new car. She'd also phoned the hospital and requested a leave of absence, claiming she needed time to regroup, to clear the cobwebs from her mind. Under the circumstances, the head of psychiatry had been more than cordial. She supposed he expected a lawsuit on his hands, but Megan didn't want revenge. She simply wanted peace. She did have mixed feelings about working at the center again. Too many reminders of Tom and now Clay occupied the place. And her trust in the people she worked with had been severed by Jones's and Parnell's actions.

Jumping into a relationship with Clay had come on the heels of Tom's death—had her feelings for him been borne out of loneliness or confusion over Clay's identity?

She didn't think so...

A wave of nausea sent her head spinning and Megan

dropped the box of clothes, struggling for composure. This was the second time this week she'd felt sick. Clutching her stomach, she went to the bathroom and opened the cabinet. The pregnancy test kit she'd purchased when she and Tom had been trying to conceive glared at her like an owl with knowing eyes from the top shelf.

Her hand trembled as she reached for it.

CLAY GRABBED A STALE doughnut from the tray, poured a thick cup of black coffee into a foam cup and ambled over to his desk. One bite into the doughnut, and he tossed it into the trash. He didn't have a taste for anything anymore. Not food or life.

He was starving for Megan.

He shoved the image of her face from his mind and tried to focus on work. "Any news on Chadburn?"

"No word," Adam said. "Seems he disappeared. Just like Hughes."

"You think he might be Hughes?"

"It's possible. He was definitely in on M-T."

Clay nodded, the words on the pages in front of him blurring. M-T was the most bizarre case he'd worked on to date. But if it hadn't been for it, he never would have met Megan.

"Have you called her?"

Clay frowned in disgust. "What, does mind reading come with marriage?"

Adam swiveled in his chair and rested his boots on his desk. "Figured it was either the woman or the shrink you've been seeing."

Clay cursed. "The shrink is simply helping me regain my memories. I'm not a lunatic."

Deep laughter rumbled from Adam's chest. "I know that, partner. But you've been through a hell of a lot lately. Being the object of a research experiment, having your memories erased, receiving a new face, all that would do a number on anyone."

"I appreciate the concern," Clay snarled, hating the fact that his friend had hit the nail on the head. "But I'm fine."

"Right. The way you've been moping around, I'd say this woman really got under your skin."

Clay shot him a dark look. "Just because you're crazy about a woman doesn't mean everyone has to get hitched."

"So, you have thought about marriage?"

Clay cursed again. Why had he said that? "Listen, Black, Megan Wells only got involved with me because she was in danger and she thought I might be her husband. She wanted a second chance with him."

"But he's dead now," Black said matter-of-factly. "And she did get involved with you. So what are you going to do about it?"

Clay shrugged, the lines on the file he needed to read blurring. He had ignored the stab of envy he'd felt at his partner's wedding a couple of months ago. But he couldn't ignore the same envy that snaked through him when he thought about Black going home to a loving wife every night. And he couldn't deny his feelings for Megan any longer.

What would Megan say if he showed up at her door? Would she want to get to know the real Clayton Fox?

THE PREGNANCY TEST was positive.

Megan toyed with a loose thread on her cotton shirt

as she waited inside the doctor's office, her mind still trying to absorb the fact that she was carrying a baby. A bitter sweetness tingled through her. Tom had wanted a baby so badly yet she had felt like a failure for not conceiving right away.

Yet now she was having another man's child.

A man she barely knew. A man who had not bothered to phone her the past two weeks.

Dr. Cronan strolled in, thumbing his goatee. He smiled, then took his office chair and folded his hands on the polished cherry desk. "Congratulations, Megan. The blood test confirms the results of your pregnancy test. It's early on, but I'd say you're about three weeks along."

Megan's heart fluttered at the thought of the tiny life growing inside her. She automatically placed a protective hand over her stomach. "I thought so."

"I understand your concern about the drugs you were given but I don't think you have anything to worry about. I checked with the lab and the dosage and short time you were under sedation shouldn't affect the fetus." He steepled his fingers. "We will of course, want to do amniocentesis when the time is right just to make sure."

"Of course." She would pray really hard until then.

A sad smile creased his eyes. "I know how much you and Tom wanted children, Megan."

She clenched her hands.

Cronan continued, "I'm sorry Tom's not here to see this."

Megan's gaze swung to his. "Actually, Dr. Cronan," she said in a shaky whisper. "The baby's not Tom's."

And she had no idea how Clayton Fox felt about children.

HIS CONVERSATION WITH BLACK chased Clay all day, sneaking up to attack him at every corner.

*What are you going to do about her?*

Nothing, had been Clay's first response.

But night had descended and once again, he headed back to his apartment alone.

The isolation he'd felt when he'd been in the hospital had been very real. Although his partner cared about him, police work had not earned him very many close friends. Or a wife.

And his family was all gone.

Remembering the deaths of his parents had been like losing them all over again.

The despair had mimicked the feelings he'd had in the hospital and caused him to reevaluate his whole life. He was tired of being alone. Tired of cold pizza and an empty bed and even more dismal lonely mornings.

The warmth of Megan's body still lingered in his mind, so real in fact that several times lately he'd reached out to pull her into his embrace during the night.

Only to wake up and realize that she wasn't there. He'd grabbed his damn pillow.

He parked his car in front of the brick house of a local breeder. When Megan's house had been broken into, he'd suggested getting her a dog. She'd mentioned that Tom had been allergic to animals, that he hadn't liked them.

A dog was one thing he could give her that Tom hadn't.

Maybe it would be the opening he would need for a fresh start with Megan.

And this time, he'd introduce her to the real Clay Fox. The man who wanted her in his bed and life, forever.

The man who wasn't her former husband as they'd once thought, but the man who wanted to be her future one.

"THANKS FOR THE CASSEROLE, Connie."

"It's not much, Megan, but I wanted you to know I was thinking about you."

"What about your job? Are you staying on at the center?"

Connie set the chicken dish down on the counter. "Yes. I'm being assigned to Dr. Ferguson. I think it will be a good fit."

"Great." Megan gave her a hug. "Kiss your little boy for me." Her hand went to her stomach again, something she'd been doing all day.

"Are you all right?" Connie asked.

"Yes, don't worry about me." I'm fine. I'm having a baby! Megan wanted to shout it to the rafters, but she held back. Until she made a decision about whether or not to tell Clay, she couldn't spill her guts to everyone else. After all, he was the father and a father had a right to know.

"Is it true that Cole Hunter turned out to be a cop?"

"Yes, his name is Clay Fox. Tom was meeting him to tell him about the memory transplant project the night he died."

Connie emitted an exasperated sound. "That story is unbelievable."

Megan laughed, a tension filled sound. Both of them knew the ordeal hadn't been funny.

"Well, I'm taking off."

Megan walked her to the door, only to find April parking in the driveway. It must be the night for visitors.

CLAY HANDED THE BREEDER his check and cradled the frisky little golden retriever in his arms as he headed to the car, but his cell phone rang just as he started the engine.

"Clay, it's Black."

"What's up?"

"Listen, I hate to tell you this but this mess isn't over. Jones was found dead in his jail cell about an hour ago."

"What?"

"He had one visitor. Logged in as Connie Blalock."

"Damn." Clay's mind raced. "Why the hell would she kill Jones?"

"I don't know. But I thought you might want to check on Megan."

"I'm on my way." Clay hung up, put his siren on top of his car, and took off, mentally reviewing the facts. Connie had been a patient of Tom's. Had suffered from depression. Had she developed a crush on Tom? Did that silver compact belong to her?

Megan had caught her shredding files. What had been inside there that she didn't want anyone to see?

He punched in Megan's number to warn her. He held his breath as he waited. Finally she answered.

"Megan, God, I'm glad you're there."

"What's wrong, Clay?"

"I don't have time to explain, but have you seen Connie?"

"Yes, she just left. She brought me dinner."

"Don't eat the food she brought. We think she may have killed Jones today."

Megan gasped.

"Just hang on and I'll be there in a minute." He hung up and took the curve on two wheels. But why would Connie kill Megan?

Because Tom had refused to leave Megan for her?

"I'VE BEEN SO WORRIED ABOUT you." April pushed inside without an invitation as Megan dropped the phone in its cradle. What was going on? Why would Connie want to hurt her? Or Jones?

April sat down at the kitchen table with a glass of iced tea. Her gaze caught the menagerie of clay pots, bowls and vases Megan had made in her pottery class the last week, and she raised a brow.

"A new hobby," Megan said.

"Therapy?"

"Something like that."

"I thought I saw you leaving the center today, but you didn't come by the psych ward. What were you doing there, Meg?"

Leave it to April not to miss a thing.

"I…" She hesitated and contemplated a lie. But she needed to tell someone other than her doctor and she and April had always been close.

"Are you thinking about coming back to work?"

"No." She poured herself a glass of tea. "I'm thinking about moving actually."

"Really?"

"Yes, it's too hard to return to the center after all that happened there. There are too many memories."

"So why did you come today?"

"I had a doctor's appointment."

April covered Megan's hand with hers. "What's wrong, Meg? Aren't you feeling well? Have you been depressed?"

"No, not exactly." Well, she had been depressed before she'd learned about the pregnancy.

"Were you in for a physical?"

"Yes." The ice clinked in her glass as she sipped her tea. "Actually, April, I went to the fertility clinic. I'm pregnant."

A frown pulled at April's mouth. "Pregnant?"

"Yes." Megan fought a smile but couldn't contain it.

April stood, eyes fixed on Megan. "I can't believe it. I thought you and Tom tried and couldn't have kids—"

"We were having trouble but the tests never indicated that I couldn't have children."

April paced across the room, hugging her purse to her side, looking agitated.

"What's wrong, April? I thought you'd be happy for me. I may be alone, but I can handle it."

"You always come out on top, don't you, Meg?"

Megan shifted, confused by the hint of anger in her friend's voice. "Things have been difficult lately but I'm trying to look on the positive side. And move on."

"Are you moving on with that man Hunter?"

Megan gulped. "His real name is Clay Fox."

"Right, he's the man responsible for Tom's death. And for getting Jonesy arrested."

"Jonesy got himself arrested because he was crazy," Megan said, disturbed by the change of conversation.

"You... You always get the men, Megan." April stomped toward her. "I don't understand it. First Tom fell for you. Head over heels. And he had an attack of conscience because of you. He almost ruined the research project."

"You knew about it?"

"Jonesy let it spill one night after too many drinks. Then that guy Cole, Clay, whatever his name was. He wasn't here a day until he was following you around like a sick puppy—"

"April, I—"

"And then Jonesy. He wanted you, too, Megan." Rage darkened April's eyes. "Or didn't you know?"

"No I—"

"He did. He even had the nerve to tell me about it while we were in bed. And after I kept his lies a secret."

Megan gasped and knocked her glass over. Tea and ice ran down the table. She reached for a cloth to wipe it up, but stopped when she saw April pull a gun from her purse. "My God, April, what are you doing?"

April's hand shook as she pointed the pistol at Megan. With her free hand, she removed a hypodermic. Megan's blood ran cold. "He told me he sat outside your house and watched you at night. He wanted you so badly he even broke in one night and watched you sleep. He stole a pair of your panties and used to imagine he was holding you when he'd touch them." April waved the gun. "Can you believe he told me that while he was having me?"

"The compact? It was yours, wasn't it?" Megan asked, the truth dawning. And April had shot at her in the car. She had ripped the covers from the bed and slashed them.

A shrill laugh escaped April. "And now you've ruined my life with Jonesy."

"Oh, God." Megan's stomach convulsed. She covered it with her hand, praying she could talk some sense into April. She didn't want to die.

And she didn't want to lose her baby.

"The fire at the hospital? Did you set that, too?"

"Figured that one out. You just didn't give up snooping. I thought if I got rid of you, Jonesy would want me."

"You killed Jones, not Connie? Because he wanted me." The magnitude of April's deception dawned. "And you killed Daryl Boyd?"

"Stupid man was part of the experiment, nothing but a prisoner, only he forgot he'd volunteered to join the project."

"Boyd was Harry Fontaine?"

"Yep." April hissed a breath and waved the hypodermic. "We couldn't believe it when he freaked over seeing Cole."

"He saw him on Nighthawk Island."

April nodded, her eyes crazed. "And that little wimp of a secretary didn't know I even took her ID. Now, I'll get rid of you, inject that stupid casserole with the same drug I gave Jones and Boyd, and Connie gets the blame."

"You need help, April." Panic raced in Megan's chest, but she had to stall. Clay was on his way.

A nasty leer lit April's face. "I need help? You're the one about to die, Meg. With you out of the way, maybe the men will finally notice me."

Megan squirmed. She would not let April drug her again and hurt her baby.

"Don't fight it and you'll go peacefully." April stalked toward her, her footsteps clicking on the floor, measured and ominous.

Megan frantically searched for something to protect herself and backed against the stove. "You can't do this, April. We were friends. Think about my baby."

"You can't have Tom's baby." In a fit of rage, April raked an arm across the counter and swept the clay pots off the counter. They hit the floor, flying, then crashed and shattered into pieces. April laughed at the mess, then lunged toward Megan.

Megan grabbed the teakettle, swung it up and flung the hot water. April yelped and fired the gun. Shots rang through the air. Megan screamed and jumped aside, ducking the spray of bullets.

# Chapter Twenty

Cole's heart thundered at the sound of gunfire. Then Megan's cry.

He quickly roped the puppy to the front porch rail and charged into the house, his weapon drawn. Night shadows hugged the wall, but the den was empty.

Scuffling noises echoed from the kitchen.

He eased around the corner.

Megan and April—not Connie—were sprawled on the floor, grappling for a gun.

"Don't move. Police."

His quiet command brought both women to a halt. Megan's face filled with relief, April's fury. April reached for the .22 but he cut her off and kicked it out of reach. "I told you not to move."

With a low cry of anger, April rolled to a sitting position and leered at Megan. Clay motioned to Megan. "You okay?"

"Yes," Megan said in a shaky voice.

"Then call the police. I'll watch your friend."

Megan nodded and stood, moving away from April with caution, then grabbed the phone. Within minutes, the Savannah Police had arrived, Adam Black in the lead.

"What the hell's going on here now?" Black asked.

"Apparently my best friend wasn't my friend at all," Megan explained, trembling.

"So, it wasn't Connie?" Black asked.

"No."

Clay winced at the pain in her voice. Megan had been hurt so many times. Black seemed to detect the same and gestured to Clay to take care of her.

"I'll lock this one up." Detective Black escorted an angry April out the door.

Clay felt Megan shaking as he pulled her into his arms.

Or maybe he was the one shaking.

"God, Megan, I damned near had a heart attack when I heard that gun go off. I thought I'd lost you for sure."

Megan had curled into his arms, but she pulled back slightly and looked up into his eyes. He saw the surprise and something else—hope? Was she glad to see him?

He ran a hand over her shimmering blond hair, over the soft skin of her cheek, then the slight tilt of her nose.

"I'm glad you're here, Clay."

His eyebrows shot up. "I missed you."

"Really?"

"Yes." And he'd brought her a present. But he wasn't ready to release her just yet to retrieve it.

She narrowed her eyes. "You missed me because of Tom's memories?"

He brushed a kiss along her temple. "No, because of mine."

She met his gaze. "You don't have amnesia anymore?"

"No," he whispered in a hoarse voice. "I hope you can forgive me for my part in Tom's death." He searched her face, looking for absolution, for any trace that she had feelings for him.

"I don't blame you, Clay. Tom died because he crossed the line. He never should have gotten involved in those projects." She licked her dry lips. "I thought you blamed Tom and me for what you went through."

"Never." Relief surged through him. He kissed her fingers, then pressed her hand against his chest. "Tom's memories of you may have brought us together, Megan. But my memories of you brought me back. And the ones we make together will keep us together if you let them."

Megan stared at Clay in surprise. Happiness mingled with love welled inside her. She could hardly believe she'd almost died at the hands of a friend a few minutes earlier, and now Clay was here, looking at her with love in his eyes. The kind of love that she'd only dreamt about.

A sly smile curved his lips as he dropped to his knees and cradled her hand in his. "I love you, Megan. Not because of Tom's memories, but because of mine. Ours. I know it's soon, and if you want to wait a while, until you get to know the real Clay Fox, I understand. But…will you marry me?"

Tears trickled down Megan's cheeks, her heart racing.

He sucked in a shaky breath, and she saw the vulnerability in his eyes. Didn't he know how she felt about him?

"I love you, too, Clay." But she knew about the baby and he didn't. Or did he? Could he somehow have found out and now he felt obligated? "Are you sure you want marriage?"

"Yes." A smile enveloped his face. "And a family and the whole works."

The slow tingle of joy spread through Megan. Until that moment, she hadn't known if what they had shared had been real. If his feelings were real. Now, the sexual tension, the emotional bond; it couldn't be more real.

She dropped to her knees in front of him, framed his face in her hands and kissed him, full and long. He responded with the fiery passion she had only known at his hands. "I would love to marry you, Clayton Fox."

He rained kisses up and down her face and neck, his throaty whisper erotic. "I could take you right here on the floor."

Megan chuckled. "I could let you, too."

A scratching sound outside filtered through her joy. Megan startled. Would she forever be jumping at any little noise? "What was that?"

"Oh, my gosh. I forgot—"

She grabbed his hand as he started to stand. She wasn't ready for him to leave her yet. Maybe never. "It's okay, Clay, I don't need a ring."

"Oh." He grinned sheepishly. "Actually I thought we'd pick that out together. But there's something else." He held up a finger. "Wait here."

Clay raced outside, and returned seconds later, carrying a small bundle of yellow fur.

"You brought me a puppy?"

"A golden retriever." He nodded, grinning all over himself as she cradled it in her arms like a baby. The puppy bounced up and down and licked her chin. "I wanted to give you something that Tom couldn't."

Megan's throat closed as she reached for his hand and placed it over her stomach. "Honey, you already have."

His gaze met hers, his pulse racing as her message sank in. "You mean…?"

"Yes, Clay," she said softly. "We're going to have a baby."

The empty black hole that had once occupied a canyon in his mind disappeared as love filled it. He took her in his arms, puppy and all, and carried her to the bedroom.

"Thank God," he whispered. "I'll never have to be alone again." He gently eased her and the dog on the bed.

"I didn't know you didn't like to be alone," Megan teased.

He ripped off his shirt. "Honey, there's a lot of things you don't know about me." Lowering his head, he kissed her softly. "Now, let's play with this puppy till he falls asleep, then I'll tell you everything you want to know about Clayton Fox."

"I hear puppies sleep a lot."

"Pregnant women need a lot of sleep, too." He nuzzled her neck. "I'll be glad to keep you company."

Megan smiled and pulled at his shirt. "You're right. And I have a feeling I'm going to need a lot of bed-rest."

\* \* \* \* \*

*Look for the next installment in Rita Herron's thrilling NIGHTHAWK ISLAND series in May 2003, THE CRADLE MISSION only from Harlequin Intrigue.*

# $ **Saving Money** $
# **Has Never Been**
# **This Easy!**

Just fill out and send in this form from any
October, November and December 2002 books
and we will send you a coupon booklet worth a
total savings of $20.00 off future purchases of
Harlequin and Silhouette books in 2003.

## **Yes! It's that easy!**

**I accept your incredible offer!**
**Please send me a coupon booklet:**

Name (PLEASE PRINT)

Address                                                    Apt. #

City                          State/Prov.              Zip/Postal Code

**In a typical month, how many**
**Harlequin and Silhouette novels do you read?**

❑ 0-2                              ❑ 3+

097KJKDNC7                                              097KJKDNDP

**Please send this form to:**
In the U.S.: Harlequin Books, P.O. Box 9071, Buffalo, NY 14269-9071
In Canada: Harlequin Books, P.O. Box 609, Fort Erie, Ontario  L2A 5X3

Allow 4-6 weeks for delivery. Limit one coupon booklet per household. Must be
postmarked no later than January 15, 2003.

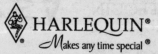